"Why don't

"Married!" Carla echoed in a startled voice. Of all the possible things, this was the last she'd expected him to say.

"Yeah, married," he said, grinning casually. "You know the routine. To have and to hold until death do us part. Shoes and rice and everything nice."

Carla caught her breath. "If this is a joke, I don't think it's very funny."

"It's not a joke," Drake said.

She thought it sounded like a wonderful idea as she savored the heat of his breath in her hair. Then she remembered the press. At one time they'd been a pack of wild, hungry dogs, and she the only bone for a hundred miles around. Marrying Drake would bring it all back. The reporters. The limelight. The questions she would never be able to answer truthfully.

Carla shuddered and reluctantly broke away from him. "It would never work," she said.

Dear Reader,

Spellbinders! That's what we're striving for. The editors at Silhouette are determined to capture your imagination and win your heart with every single book we publish. Each month, six Special Editions are chosen with *you* in mind.

Our authors are our inspiration. Writers such as Nora Roberts, Tracy Sinclair, Kathleen Eagle, Carole Halston and Linda Howard—to name but a few—are masters at creating endearing characters and heartrending love stories. Their characters are everyday people—just like you and me—whose lives have been touched by love, whose dreams and desires suddenly come true!

So find a cozy, quiet place to read, and create your own special moment with a Silhouette Special Edition.

Sincerely,

The Editors
SILHOUETTE BOOKS

SANDRA DEWAR
Conquer the Memories

Silhouette Special Edition

Published by Silhouette Books New York

America's Publisher of Contemporary Romance

To my husband, my favorite hero
And Bonnie, my favorite heroine
All my love and infinite thanks.

SILHOUETTE BOOKS
300 East 42nd St., New York, N.Y. 10017

Copyright © 1987 by Sandra Dewar

ISBN: 0-373-09405-1

First Silhouette Books printing September 1987

America's Publisher of Contemporary Romance

Printed in the U.S.A.

SANDRA DEWAR

wanted to be a writer since the age of ten. Along the way she had other careers, such as being a nanny in France and catching guppies in Trinidad, Venezuela and Martinique. She hates housekeeping, claiming that *dust* and *iron* are four-letter words, but she loves gourmet cooking and all forms of needlework. She is married to a professor of physics, and perhaps as a result, claims that her daughter, Colleen, has all the energy and destructive power of an atomic bomb.

Ventura Frwy   Eagle Rock Pasadena   Lake Arrowhead
                                           Colorado Frwy
Beverly Hills   Lanning
                                                Mountain Cottages   Pomona

         Santa Monica Frwy

                                                                  LOS ANGELES
                                                                  AND VICINITY

                                   PACIFIC OCEAN

CALIFORNIA

                                                        Anaheim

Big Sur

                    Pasedena

                                    Lake Arrowhead

Beverly Hills

                              Anaheim

Underlined places are fictitious.

Chapter One

The house wasn't at all what Carla had expected.

The wrought-iron gate at the entrance, the undulating acres of verdant lawn, had all been typical Beverly Hills glitz, but the house was—well—the house was a surprise. Carla Foster switched off the car ignition and stared at the white clapboard colonial-style house. Green shutters framed the windows and matched the green front door and a narrow line of green trim under the gray slate roof. A jacaranda tree stretched feathery green arms, weeping purple blossoms onto a black Firebird parked in the keyhole-shape driveway. Pink, purple and white petunias splashed color along the sides of the slate walkway.

The ambience was peaceful, conservative, and decidedly unpretentious.

Could this really be the home of rock star Drake Lanning?

She hadn't wanted to do this interview. She'd fought tooth and nail to get out of it. But Elizabeth Rice, Carla's boss and the social worker responsible for Bobby's case, had insisted, claiming she had another appointment at that time that she couldn't break. Anyway, Elizabeth had added tartly, it was time for Carla to get over her aversion to anything and anyone connected with the music business.

Elizabeth might be right, but that wasn't going to make this any easier.

Carla opened the briefcase sitting on the seat next to her and looked in her case file to recheck the address. She'd made no mistake: this was the home of Drake Lanning.

She tilted the rearview mirror and observed her image in its reflection. A discreet pink color enhanced the gentle fullness of her lips. The teal-blue eye shadow and dark-brown mascara framing her blue eyes were so subtle that they were barely detectable.

Her long blond hair was parted on the left and gathered in a dignified chignon. As she smoothed back a loose tendril, she made sure that the hairstyle covered the long scar on her scalp where her hair wouldn't grow. It did. Now if only a hairstyle could hide the emotional scars, too, she thought wryly to herself.

Would Drake recognize her? Few people realized that the quiet young woman in the severely tailored suits had once had her picture featured regularly on newspaper pages all over the world. Privacy—the right to do whatever she wanted without anyone giving a damn—was such a luxury: a luxury she'd never known until she was eighteen. It was the reason she'd changed her name. It was the reason she avoided everyone who had anything to do with music. Until today.

Carla snapped her briefcase shut and silently told herself to forget about everything but what she was there to do. Which led her back to the question she'd asked when Elizabeth had first handed her the case file. Why did Drake Lanning want to adopt a fifteen-year-old boy? In the motivation letter included with his application for adoption, Drake had written that he wanted to give Bobby Dixon a break. What did that mean?

Why would a man who was in the public eye a ''celebrity,'' who purportedly lived in the fast lane, want to tie himself down by adopting a fifteen-year-old?

Carla slammed the car door shut with unnecessary force. Smoothing down the skirt of her white linen suit, she strode the gray slate walkway with confidence. Drake Lanning and his homey little abode had given her an initial shock; the next surprise, though, would be all hers.

She had arrived an hour earlier than scheduled for the appointment. It was a dirty trick, but Carla had discovered long ago that it sometimes elicited interesting results. Usually she just interrupted a last-minute housecleaning, but one time she had interrupted a last-minute cocaine deal.

Adjusting her eyeglasses on her nose, Carla took a moment to calm herself before announcing her arrival. She'd interviewed people wanting to adopt kids hundreds of times. So why did she feel so edgy? Stifling an urge to get back in her car, Carla lifted the shiny brass knocker and pounded aggressively.

She waited, her heart hammering like a piston valve in high gear. Why had Elizabeth insisted she do this interview? Elizabeth knew Carla's reasons for shunning the music world; knew that she feared someone would recognize her.

Carla jerked herself out of her reverie as the door swung open. A curvaceous young brunette with a yellow bath towel wrapped around her middle answered the door. She yawned heartily, then said, "We already gave."

"I'm sure you did," Carla replied in dulcet tones. She thrust a foot in the closing door. "I'm here to see Mr. Lanning."

"You'll have to come back later. He's in the shower." The woman began to look annoyed as Carla refused to budge.

"I'll wait in the living room, if you don't mind."

The brunette readjusted the towel, which was starting to unwind. Shrugging indifferently, she turned to walk away. They both were still in the hallway when Carla heard the sound of bare feet slapping against the tiled floor.

"Hey, Angie, you'd better get a move on. I don't want that battle-ax of a social worker finding you here."

Carla recognized the throaty voice from his records. Not that she owned any of his records, but she couldn't turn on the radio without hearing his music. She pivoted on her high heels. Drake Lanning stood a few feet away, wrapped in a yellow bath towel that matched the brunette's.

Carla had seen pictures of Drake on the covers of magazines, but still, the reality was a shock. He was tall and powerfully built, his body a relief map of bone, sinuous muscle and tanned skin.

His lean, finely sculpted face wasn't handsome. It was too compelling, too raw and vital for such a mundane word. *Sexy...earthy...primitive* were more descriptive adjectives. Carla sucked in a gulp of air and lightly said, "My, my, isn't this cozy? His and Hers bath-towel wear. Did I interrupt something interesting or are you just practicing for a fashion show?"

"Who are you?" Drake demanded, taking a menacing step forward. "If you're a reporter..."

"I'm Miss Foster, that battle-ax of a social worker," Carla replied with false brightness, willing herself to look at his face and not his physique. "I'm sorry I'm a trifle early. I hope it's not inconvenient."

"Oh, not a bit," he replied, his tone belying his words. He flung a glance at the brunette, and said, "Angie, you'd better get dressed and go. I'll call you soon." His gaze swung back to Carla. "Why don't you sit down in the living room? I'll join you as soon as I'm dressed." He raked a hand through glistening, wet brown curls. Brown eyes the same color as his hair suddenly danced as he extended a hand invitingly. "Unless you'd prefer to interview me like this?"

Carla flicked her eyes downward, then wished she hadn't. The towel had slipped, exposing pelvic bones, a flat stomach, and a mass of wiry brown hair leading from the towel line up to his throat. Carla hoped she wasn't blushing. Glancing up, she saw him trying to suppress a smile. "I'll wait for you in the living room," she managed.

It's his body that has you so flustered, she told herself as she walked away. And his eyes. And his smile. And his nearly nude state. As her heels clattered on the tiles, she reminded herself that she had the upper hand. He would have to do some fancy talking to explain why he'd had a woman with him at this time of the morning.

Drake, who was hurriedly getting dressed in his bedroom, was cursing himself for having let Angie spend the night. How could he have overslept on such an important morning? It must have been all that wine he'd consumed the night before. He'd been as nervous as a bridegroom about the interview. And now he may have blown it without ever saying a word.

He bent down on his knees and peered under the bed for the mate to his leather sandal. Neatness had never been one of his virtues. If Dolores, the maid who came in the afternoon to cook and clean, didn't constantly lecture him about picking up after himself, the house would be a disaster.

The matching sandal was nowhere to be found, so he settled for his red and gray running shoes instead.

To hell with dressing up, he told himself; she can take me as I am. He hated being rushed. He hated being late. He always arrived at his performances hours early. And now he found himself both late and rushed . . . and on the defensive. He picked up the orphan sandal and pitched it across the room. The shoe made a satisfying *ker-thunk* as it slammed against the wall.

He told himself to calm down. It wouldn't be smart to let the cool blonde in the living room know that she'd managed to upset him. He pictured her in her white linen suit and matching high heels, surrounded by a discreetly sophisticated perfume.

She wasn't his type of woman at all. He preferred a more down-to-earth woman, not a "touch me not" beauty. So why had he felt instantly attracted to her? Even stranger—why had he felt an eerie spark of recognition when he'd first seen her standing in the hallway?

He pulled on a blue shirt and told himself that Miss Foster didn't matter. Bobby was the only person who mattered. He had to help Bobby. Looking at Bobby was like looking at himself at fifteen. He had been just as wild, just as cocky, just as talented . . . and just as hell-bent for self-destruction. Folk musician Tyler Gunther had helped straighten Drake out. He had seen Drake's talent and his desperate hunger to be somebody. Tyler was dead now, but his memory lived on for Drake. And now it was Drake's turn to return the favor to another confused kid. He had to help Bobby get his chance. And Miss Foster had better not try to stop him.

Carla sat in the living room trying to ignore its reminders of her past. The musical paraphernalia seemed to mock her. She had her back to the piano, but it was impossible to ignore the battered Gibson guitar slung carelessly across an overstuffed chair—not to mention the framed medieval music featured on the walls, and the stacks of sheet music on the floor.

Once again, Drake Lanning had surprised her. Instead of plush wall-to-wall carpeting, there was brown Mexican tile, with lots of Navaho rugs to break the monotony. The couches were overstuffed beige tweed—not fancy, but comfortable. Along the east wall was a bookcase jumbled with books. The opposite wall was all sunlight and French windows and opened onto a tropically landscaped pool patio.

She readjusted the glasses digging into the bridge of her nose. Glasses were a nuisance, especially for someone with perfect vision, but they were worth the sacrifice. She didn't want Drake Lanning—or anyone else, for that matter—to look at her and gasp, "My God, you're Carla Fox!"

That had happened only once in her five years of being a social worker. That time she'd managed to persuade the prospective adoptive parents to keep quiet.

There were footsteps on the tile. She looked down at the sheaf of papers on her lap and pretended to read. She already had enough information on Drake to rival the FBI's secret files. She knew that his yearly salary was larger than the gross national product of some third-world countries, that his mother's maiden name was Casey. She knew how much each of his three homes were worth and that he'd had a tonsillectomy at the age of five. She knew everything about the man—and nothing about the man inside.

But he was all man, of that she was sure. He came striding into the room in tight blue jeans slung low on lean hips. A blue short-sleeved cotton shirt showed off his broad shoulders and muscular forearms.

"Miss Foster." He greeted her with a show of dazzling white teeth. "Can I get you something to drink? Coffee? Tea? Or juice?"

"No, thank you," she replied stiffly, noticing that the same brown curl that was always out of place in his photographs was drooping across his forehead in a familiar fashion.

She watched as Drake sauntered over to the couch and sat down next to her. Forcing her voice to sound calm and businesslike, she asked, "Tell me, Mr. Lanning, why do you want to adopt Bobby?"

He looked at her thoughtfully as he brushed the curl away from his forehead. It sprang back immediately. "It's all in the application. I want to give Bobby a break. He hasn't had many. I figure he's about due for one."

Carla groped for something to say. His woodsy cologne assaulted her senses and his leg was nearly touching her. Why did he have to sit so near? The chair next to her would have been the obvious place for him to sit. Carla had to crane her neck to look at him, or turn her body, which put her leg against his. He was putting her at a distinct disadvantage.

He was putting her at a distinct disadvantage. Of course. The man was no fool. Carla crossed her legs and cautiously inched away. Reminding herself that there was no reason for her to feel intimidated, she said, "Wanting to help is a noble sentiment. But I find it a little hard to believe. What's in this for you?"

"Does there have to be something in it for me?"

Smiling politely, she said, "There's always something in it for us."

He nodded. "You're right, of course. Tell me, why did you become a social worker?"

She was startled by his question, but could see no reason not to reply. "Because I wanted to help people."

The smug look on his face made her realize that she'd made his point for him. He flashed her a smile and said, "I guess you and I have a lot in common. I want to help Bobby. You want to help people."

She bent her head momentarily to peruse the notes sitting on her lap. Then she raised her head and inquired, "How did you meet Bobby and become interested in him?"

Drake ran his fingers through his hair and looked up at the ceiling for a moment as he remembered. "He was hanging around the recording-studio door one night, so stoned out of his mind that he couldn't even remember his name. He'd just run away from one of those foster homes you people are so fond of sticking him into, and he seemed determined to OD on drugs rather than go back. I took him home, sobered him up, and tried to talk some sense into him.''

"And did you talk some sense into him?"

Drake shrugged. "He's stayed clean ever since, and that was two months ago. I can't make any promises, but I want to give it a try."

"That's a praiseworthy sentiment," Carla said, pushing the glasses back on her nose. "But do you have any idea of the enormous responsibility you'll be taking on yourself if you adopt Bobby?"

"I have an idea. After all, I was a kid once myself." He leaned back on the couch and folded his arms behind his head. A leg sprawled out, brushing Carla's thigh. "I figure that's a good start."

Carla found the touch of their bodies distracting. She thought about moving over, but a large pillow blocked her way. "Now about the, er—" Carla hesitated "—lady I met this morning. What role does she play in your life? Is she just a friend? Or are you planning to marry her?"

"The, er, lady—" he cleared his throat "—is just a friend. I have no plans for marrying her."

"I see," Carla said, taking notes. "Do you have many close friends? Or is she the only one?"

"Miss Foster," Drake said in shocked tones, "that's a very personal question."

"Sorry," she said sweetly, grateful finally to have found a question that nettled him. "These kinds of questions are just part of my job."

"And you love every minute of it," he murmured softly.

"I beg your pardon? I didn't quite catch that last comment."

"Good," he countered, flashing her a beguiling smile. "But if it's gory details you want, it's gory details you'll get. I admit I'm no monk. I like a woman in my life. I like a woman in my bed, too. But only one woman at a time. I suppose I'm the shy type. I don't like crowds."

As she scribbled this down, he continued, "I know Angie's being here this morning looks bad. But I promise you I know how to be discreet. I wouldn't dream of exposing Bobby to such activities when he comes to live with me."

"If he comes to live with you," Carla corrected smoothly. Lifting a hand to readjust her glasses, she went on, "It says on your application here that you've never been married. May I ask why not?"

He waved a hand. "Just lucky, I guess."

Carla shuffled through her papers. "Why are you against marriage? You state that your parents are still together. Are they unhappily married?"

"Not at all. They still hold hands after thirty-five years of marriage. I just don't like the idea of being tied down."

"Adopting Bobby's going to tie you down," Carla warned.

"That's different," he said confidently.

"In what way?" she shot back.

He sprang up from the couch and walked over to the French windows. With his back to the room, he replied in a low but intense voice: "I already told you. I care about Bobby. He's important to me."

"And you don't care about the women in your life? They're not important?"

"Good Lord," he lamented, turning around. Under his breath, he muttered, "Why do I have to get stuck with a terminal virgin for a social worker?"

"I don't believe you said that," Carla retorted in a stunned voice.

"Neither do I," Drake replied, realizing his error the second the words fell from his mouth. He flashed her a contrite smile. "Look, I'm sorry I said that, Miss Foster. I was totally out of line. We seem to be getting off on the wrong foot. Why don't you go outside, knock on the door, and we'll start all over again?"

"I'm afraid it's a little late for that," Carla replied dryly.

It seemed like a miracle to Carla that he managed to stuff his hands into his tight jean pockets, but he did. As he began to pace the room, he turned his head and regarded her thoughtfully. "Look, I don't claim to be a saint. But I'm no sinner, either. Someone once told me that my heart's as big as my mouth. I guess they were right. Can't we just let bygones be bygones?"

"That's easy for you to say. Nobody ever called you a terminal virgin."

He couldn't help grinning. "They'd be lying if they did."

She frowned at him. "The shoe doesn't fit here, either."

"I'm so happy for you."

"I'm thrilled."

"I'm glad you are."

The man is insufferable, she thought, sorely tempted to wad her interview sheet into a ball and throw it at him. So why did she feel an urge to show him that she wasn't the inhibited virgin he imagined her to be? And why had she felt compelled to tell him she wasn't?

She shoved the glasses back on her nose and tried to regain her composure.

Drake walked toward Carla and dropped onto the chair next to her. Crossing one leg over the other, he said, "I know. Let's act like we just met. You ask me all your questions and I'll pretend I'm *Father Knows Best*."

"You don't strike me as the *Father Knows Best* type."

"Sorry," he apologized, slinking low in his chair. "Wrong series. I'll pretend I'm *Bachelor Father*. At least he got to swing a little."

She sighed in exasperation. "Mr. Lanning, this isn't a situation comedy. We can sit here and fling witticisms at one another all morning. But that's not going to get the job done. We're just wasting our time."

"Okay, okay." He threw up his hands in mock surrender. "Ask me your questions and I'll tell you no lies."

She heaved another sigh and pushed back her glasses. Then she straightened her notes and continued, "We've already discussed Bobby's weakness for drugs. But what about you? Drugs and musicians seem to go hand in hand. You can't pick up a newspaper without reading about some musician getting arrested for drugs. What kind of drugs do you use? And please feel free to be honest. This interview won't go further than the two of us."

"You don't know much about me, do you?" he remarked, drumming his fingers on the armrest of the chair. "I'm the cleanest thing around. You're welcome to search the house if you want," he offered with a grand sweep of his hand. "But I'll warn you—the only drugs you'll find are aspirin and some decongestants for my allergies. I don't do drugs. I may be a rock musician, but I'm not stupid."

She believed him. She didn't know why, but she did. Perhaps it was the fit condition of his body that told her he was telling the truth. If he went to so much effort to keep in shape, surely he wouldn't ruin it all with drugs.

"Another thing that has me worried," she began, "is what's going to happen to Bobby when you're away on tour."

"If Bobby doesn't have school, he'll come with me. I'm a great believer in families staying together. If he's in school, he'll stay with my parents."

"Are your parents agreeable to this?" Carla questioned sharply.

"Are you kidding? My mom's main complaint in life is that none of her four kids have given her grandchildren. Now she'll finally have one. She's already planning menus for the poor kid. If Bobby doesn't come back fifty pounds heavier, I'll be surprised."

"I see," she said thoughtfully. "Please tell me more about your parents. What was it like growing up with them?"

"Terrific. My parents are very special people who absolutely live for their kids. We never had much money, but that didn't seem to matter. All my friends with their rich parents and fancy houses seemed to prefer to hang out at our house." He grinned. "My mom was a better cook. Better still, she didn't complain about the racket we made with our instruments."

"Did it bother you not having any money?"

He shrugged. "It bothered me as much as it would bother any kid."

It was time for her to drop her bombshell. She'd been waiting from the start of the interview for the appropriate time. She'd wanted him relaxed. "Is not having any money the reason you stole that car?"

She knew she'd made a direct hit the moment the words dropped from her mouth. His eyes narrowed and his mouth turned grim. The words he spit back at her were rapid and short. "How did you hear about that?"

"Just lucky, I guess," she replied, quoting him. She wasn't about to admit that her sometime boyfriend,

Jerry O'Roarke, had been the young policeman responsible for arresting him at the time.

"I've got to hand it to you, lady," he said, emphasizing the last word. "You're more efficient than the *gossip rags*. Even they haven't managed to dig up that piece of dirt."

Uncrossing one leg from the other, she tucked her legs under and pulled her skirt down to her knees. "Do you want to tell me about it?"

"Not really. But I guess I don't have any choice." He grimaced as he raked a hand through his hair. He wasn't often at loss for words, but this time he had to grope. "When I was sixteen, I was like a lot of kids: I was hell on wheels. I thought I knew everything there was to know. I even thought I could hang around a tough bunch of kids and still stay clean. Then one day things exploded in my face. The cops stopped me while I was driving a friend's car. At least I thought it was my friend's car. I found out too late. My friend had stolen the car."

"Some friend."

He shrugged. "I was very young—and very foolish. And very, very fortunate. The man who owned the car dropped the charges. Since I was a minor and it was my first offense, the authorities erased my arrest record."

"You were fortunate," Carla agreed, tapping her pen thoughtfully against the stack of papers sitting on her lap.

"I guess you could say that. Funny luck, that's me. The damnedest things happen, and I always end up on top." He smiled roguishly. "It's one of my favorite places to be."

Deciding to ignore the possible connotations of that sally, Carla said briskly, "Mr. Lanning, I want to reassure you. You seemed upset when I asked you about this incident with the car. Rest assured, your secret is still safe. I promise you I would never repeat such a story, and my written report is strictly confidential."

He shrugged. "I'm not worried that people won't buy my records if they find out. I just like to keep my private life private."

"It will remain private, I can assure you," Carla replied as she began to stuff papers back into her briefcase. The locks made a satisfying click as she snapped them shut. "That about concludes our interview, Mr. Lanning. Thank you. We'll be in touch."

They both stood up. Drake accepted the hand she offered him and said, "I promise you I'll take good care of Bobby. You'll never have reason to regret saying yes to my application."

Carla headed for the door. The interview had gone well, and she was pleased she'd managed to keep her cool. More important, he hadn't recognized her. She stopped at the door to say goodbye once again.

He opened the door for her. Just as she stepped out, he remarked, "One more thing, Miss Foster. Have we ever met before? It's been bugging me all day. Your face seems so familiar. I wish I could place where I've seen you before."

Carla turned and gave him a practiced, cool stare. Only the widening of her eyes behind the tortoiseshell frames betrayed her anxiety. She replied smoothly, "You must be mistaking me for someone else, Mr. Lanning. We've never met before." She pivoted and strode swiftly down the slate walkway.

Chapter Two

The piano had been taunting Carla all day.

It reminded her of a scene from an old Disney cartoon. Any moment she expected the battered old upright to grow legs and march over and attack her. She could see its scarred mahogany front suddenly sprouting bug eyes and a leering mouth. At the same time the piano would burst forth with a thundering Wagnerian tune, its black and white keys tripping down the keyboard like an old-fashioned player piano.

She had forsaken music years ago; why wouldn't music leave her alone?

Carla shoved back the glasses that had slouched low on her nose. Despite her anxiety, she kept on reading out loud, her voice schooled to a calm, soporific tone.

She was perched on top of a rickety old stool in the second-floor recreation room of the orphanage. A dozen children sat cross-legged on the floor around her, their faces wide-eyed and believing as she read them the story of Bambi.

Her voice cracked. She could never get to the part about Bambi's mother disappearing without being moved. She felt tears welling in her eyes. She blinked them away as she snapped the book shut.

"That's enough for today," she announced. "Time for your afternoon nap."

There was the usual chorus of protests, but no one realized that she'd cut their reading time short by five minutes. She couldn't go on. She felt too drained, too unsettled. Standing up, she wondered once again what was wrong with her. She'd been edgy all day.

Was she feeling guilty because she'd turned down Drake Lanning's application for adoption? No, that couldn't be. It had been the best decision. It had been the only decision. Hadn't it?

Eager hands clutched at Carla's skirt as she guided the noisy children toward their sleeping quarters. She bent down and picked up recalcitrant Tommy Greer who repeated over and over "I want mo' Bambi."

"Mona will read more tonight," Carla promised, giving Tommy a big hug. She heard the creak of heavy footsteps on the stairs. Who could that be? she wondered. Elizabeth was out having lunch and Carrie had called in sick.

"Mona doesn't read as good as you," Karen Moore, a tiny four-year-old confided. "She doesn't make all those funny noises."

Carla heard footsteps on the landing and looked up. Drake Lanning was walking toward her, looking more like a lawyer than a rock star in his tan linen suit. Drake had been stunning in jeans, even more exciting in a yellow bath towel, but today he was magnificent. His wide, powerfully muscular shoulders and tall, lean frame set off the expensive tailored suit to perfection. A discreet and conservative beige-and-blue plaid tie made a tasteful contrast against his blue shirt.

His language, though, was neither discreet nor conservative. Pushing away the front of his jacket, he planted his hands on his hips and said, "Well, if it isn't the sanctimonious bureaucrat herself."

"I gather you want to speak with me," Carla said coolly, propelling the children toward their room. "You'll have to wait until I've finished putting the children to bed."

"I'll help," he offered.

Her voice was icy. "Your help, Mr. Lanning, is not necessary, nor will it make me return any faster."

"For your information, Miss Foster," he replied, his voice heavy with sarcasm, "there was no ulterior motive in my offer. I just happen to like kids. All kids." Carla raised an eyebrow in a doubting fashion, but said nothing as Drake followed her.

The preschoolers' dormitory was a large room with iron-frame beds lining opposite walls. Each child had a small bureau and a wooden box for his toys. The walls were colorfully decorated with pictures of cartoon characters and the children's own drawings.

Carla was amazed to find that Drake hadn't lied; he did like kids. And what was more telling, the kids liked him. It had taken Carla weeks to win the trust of some of these battered and abused children, but with Drake it took only a matter of minutes. He was an enchanter.

Drake had vitality; he was full of life and good humor. As Carla watched him tell the children the story of Jason, a cowardly robot—a story he was obviously making up as he went along—she couldn't help but be envious. To be that open and joyous must be wonderful. But she knew that she could never be like him; her cautious reserve had been ingrained the hard way, and at an early age. It was now as much a part of her as her blond hair and blue eyes.

She looked at her watch and was surprised to find that it was nearly two o'clock. Time had galloped by. She broke in, "Thank you, Mr. Lanning, for entertaining us today. I hate to spoil all the fun, but it's nap time."

"Aww," everyone complained, including Drake. Carla cast Drake a stern look and he relented with an engaging smile. Picking up a pouting child, Drake made a great show of carrying him to bed and tucking him under the covers. Then he said, "Miss Foster's right, you know. You'll never get to be big and strong and handsome like me—" he flashed her a mischievous look "—if you don't take naps. I'll be by

later this week to see if you've been taking my advice.
And next time I'll bring my guitar."

This was greeted with many loud shouts of approval. Waving kisses goodbye to everyone, Drake
followed Carla as she exited through the doorway.

The minute they were out of the room Carla took
Drake by the arm and dragged him down the hallway
to the recreation room. She slammed the door shut,
once they were inside. "That was a very cruel thing
you just did," she practically yelled.

"What?" he replied, mystified.

"Promising those poor children you'd come back—
and with a guitar, no less. They've already been
handed enough disappointments in their short lives.
Why do you have to hand them another one?"

There was a menacing glint in his brown eyes as he
said, "Just what makes you so sure I won't show?"

She knew he was angry, but she was too angry herself to care. Crossing her arms over her chest, she said
evenly, "Oh, I'm sure your intentions are good—at
the moment. But somehow you'll never manage to get
around to doing what you've promised."

He cocked an eyebrow. "Somebody must have disappointed you pretty badly as a kid to make you such
a cynic."

She tossed her head. "I'm not a cynic; I'm a real-
ist. I've seen your type before."

"And what makes you the world's expert on my
type?" he inquired curtly.

Carla looked up at him. Standing just a few feet
away from her, he looked very large and very power-

ful. She told herself she wasn't afraid. After all, what could he do to her? Beat her up? All she had to do was scream and a dozen children would come running down the hall to rescue her. She lifted her chin. "Instinct, I guess. You get to know people in my business."

"And you call yourself a social worker!" Drake's voice lashed across the room like a whip. "A social worker's supposed to be a human being, not a computer. They're supposed to believe in people. I offer to help Bobby and what do you do? Turn down my application. Tell me, Miss Foster, why did you turn me down?"

She shrugged. "I didn't think you'd be good for Bobby."

"You didn't think I'd be good for Bobby," he mimicked. "And what do you think is good for Bobby? Living in this institutional dump? Being cared for by a bunch of robots like you? For the first time in Bobby's life he has someone who cares about him. And you won't let him go. You won't even give him a chance."

Be calm, Carla told herself. In a placating tone she usually saved for the preschoolers, she said, "Look, I realize you're upset. And I'm sorry. You seem to think that caring about Bobby will make you the perfect parent. Life isn't that simple. I only wish it was. Cases come through my hands every day of parents who care for their children—and the parents have done the children immeasurable harm."

She'd thought her words would appease him, but they seemed to have the opposite effect. "Is that all Bobby is to you? A case? A number?" He put his hands on his hips as he raged at her. "A manila folder to be shoved back into a filing cabinet someday? How much time have you devoted to the poor kid? Do you know him at all?"

"Of course I know him. I've read his case file. We've had interviews—"

"I'm not talking about interviews," he snapped. "I'm talking about knowing him. What makes him tick. What makes him rebel. What's made him run away from every foster home that you people have ever thrown him into."

Her voice rang out shrilly, sounding sharp to even her ears, as she retorted, "Mr. Lanning, I do my best. I'd love to get to know every kid in this orphanage, but I don't have the time or the energy. Good Lord, I'm responsible for fifty children! Do you have any idea the amount of work that entails?"

"You have the nerve to talk about time and energy when a kid's life is at stake," he countered, pointing an angry finger at her. "I'm supposed to meekly put up with your veiled insults and innuendos about my personal life, but look at you! What do you know about lonely kids? What do you know about rejection? For that matter, what do you know about suffering? I'm sure the only kind of suffering you've ever felt is the embarrassment of running your panty hose."

With one quick step he was standing in front of her, a tower of indignation and rage. His next words were fierce and crushing. "A social worker's supposed to have a heart. I picked Bobby off the streets when he was so high he couldn't tell his head from a cloud in the sky. He's been in five foster homes since his parents dumped him and he's run away from every one. Your orphanage has labeled him incorrigible. I could straighten him out if you'd just give me a chance. He's crazy about music and he's damn good at it. He thinks I'm some kind of super hero, so he listens to me. I want to help Bobby—but you won't give me a chance."

Carla felt the past closing in on her. She lowered her head so he wouldn't see the tears welling in her eyes. A lump clogged her throat and she knew she didn't dare speak. If she did, her voice would break.

The harshness of his words echoed in her brain, tormenting her. *What do you know about lonely kids?* Oh Lord, if only he knew. *What do you know about rejection?* She knew more than he did—of that she was sure. The last question was the most ironic of all: *What do you know about suffering?* Anger suddenly surged up and flooded her veins. She, who had been beaten and tormented as a child, now had to suffer this from him. How dare he be so self-righteous! How dare he judge her!

Only the years of hard-won self-control managed to save her from an outburst of tears and a loss of dignity. Raising her head, she tilted her chin proudly, saying, "My personal life isn't under discussion. But your personal life is. Getting angry with me isn't going to help your case one bit. So you might as well throw in your His and Hers towel set and admit defeat.''

For a moment he just stood there, trying to contain his temper. She was surprised when she finally saw him nod at her coolly. Drake Lanning was hotheaded, she decided, but he did show signs of being sensible. She couldn't help admiring him for that.

"I'll go quietly," he said in a low voice, "If you just answer my question: Why did you turn me down? I would have been good for Bobby. I was his big chance."

"You keep harping on Bobby's big chance," she snapped back. "His big chance for what? A life in the fast lane? Enough sex and drugs and rock and roll to burn him out by the age of twenty?"

Anger glittered in Drake's eyes. His next words were more resigned than angry. "That's not my style at all. You turned me down—" his voice broke momentarily "—you turned *us* down without your even knowing me."

Then he was gone. Carla suppressed the urge to run after him and apologize. He'd looked so desolate, so shaken as he'd stormed out of the room. She hadn't realized Bobby was that important to him. Had she completely misjudged Drake? Did his casual attitude hide a heart that really cared?

The old upright piano against the west wall mocked her as before. "Oh, leave me alone," she cried, half expecting the piano to slink away like a scolded dog.

Control. She'd worked so long and hard to obtain it. Now it seemed to be slipping away. The psychologists were right. Repression did horrible things to a person's mind. Look what she'd just done to Drake and Bobby.

With eyes fixed upon the piano, she slowly crossed the room. She stopped abruptly when she reached the instrument, and she gazed at it for a long moment. It had been so long since she'd really looked at a piano. So long since she'd felt the cool ivory and black keys heat up with passion beneath her touch.

Oh, she still played songs for the children when they insisted. But she deliberately kept her emotions out of it. Nowadays, her renditions of childhood tunes were mechanical and lifeless, worlds apart from the way she used to sing and play.

Once, she had lived for music. Once, she would happily have died for music. But her mother had died instead.

Carla let her fingers trickle along the keys, enjoying the discordant yet clear sounds that issued forth. As she sat down on the bench, she felt a surprising eagerness for the coming reunion. Lovingly, she stroked the keys. She smiled as she heard the golden mellow tone, and felt overwhelmingly grateful that Elizabeth was too much of a music lover to let the piano go untuned.

Her hands felt stiff and unpracticed, and to her ears, the music sounded amateurish. But it was such a great pleasure to be playing again that she didn't care. All the songs that had remained unsung suddenly came bubbling forth, like spring water in a long-frozen stream.

There were so many songs she wanted to play that she didn't know quite where to begin. She started with an old Gershwin favorite, one she had learned long ago as a child.

For the first time in years she felt alive. She was in touch with what she loved: music. It had always been her joy and her retreat. It was the natural outlet for her reserved, shy nature.

Why had she given it up? From fear? From guilt? From a misguided feeling that giving up what she loved most would erase the past?

Stupid girl, she scolded herself. The past and its secrets would always haunt her. But why should she let the past overwhelm the future?

Drake slung his suit jacket over his shoulder as he closed the door to Elizabeth's downstairs office. His funny luck had just shown its face. When he'd come raging down the stairs after talking with Carla, he'd run—quite literally—into Carla's boss, Elizabeth Rice, in the hallway.

One of the disadvantages of fame was that people always knew who you were. This time it had worked to Drake's advantage. Elizabeth had greeted him cheerfully and said, "Mr. Lanning! I've been wanting to speak with you for days. Do you have time to step into my office and talk for a few minutes?"

Of course he had time, he had assured her as he made a quick calculation. Perhaps if he appealed to

Elizabeth—Bobby's social worker and the head of the organization—she would change Carla's decision on the adoption.

He had turned on his charm. He had cajoled and sweetly begged. Still, he was startled when Elizabeth said briskly, "I agree with you wholeheartedly, Mr. Lanning. You would be a good influence on Bobby. I can tell that from the change I've seen in him already. Not only have his attitude and his schoolwork improved, but for the first time in his life he seems happy. Because of this, I've decided to overturn Carla's decision and recommend that Bobby be put in your care as a foster child until the courts can make the adoption final."

"Why, thank you, that's great," Drake said, pleased but surprised.

"There's only one little favor I ask of you," Elizabeth said, folding her hands together. "Will you tell Carla of my decision yourself? I believe you'll find her upstairs."

"Of course," Drake agreed, puzzled by her request. It was all very strange. Almost as strange as the piano music he'd heard filtering through the walls of the creaking old house. It had been a hodgepodge of eras and sounds—a little classical, a little popular, a little folk. And the musician was rusty, he could tell by the way the music would start, falter, stop, then start again.

His long legs took the worn-carpeted stairs two at a time. As he ascended, the music grew louder. The more Drake heard, the more curious he became. There

was passion and pathos in the playing, despite the false
starts and mistakes.

By the time he reached the top of the staircase, he
had completely forgotten that he was supposed to be
looking for Miss Foster. Instead, he had decided to
discover who this eloquent, gifted, and painfully out-
of-practice musician was. Remembering the old piano
in the recreation room, he decided the music must be
coming from there.

He strode purposefully down the hallway, stopping
momentarily when he came to the closed door. He
thought about knocking, but decided against it.
Opening the door quietly, he stepped inside.

Afternoon sunlight cast dusky shadows on the
woman sitting at the piano bench. There was no other
light. She had her back to him, and her blond hair had
tumbled loose on her shoulders. He tiptoed across the
room and regarded the intense figure hunched over the
piano.

It's Miss Foster, he realized. But where did she learn
to play the piano? And where did she learn to sing like
that?

She was good—very good, he thought admiringly.
And she sounded just like Carla Fox. She had the
same clear, husky vibrato, the same impressive com-
mand of both high and low ranges. Even more incredible was her ability to communicate the wistful,
haunting sadness for which Carla Fox had been so famous.

He edged over to the piano, where Miss Foster was
too wrapped up in her music to even notice him. She'd

cast off her eyeglasses, he noted, and left them resting on the piano.

He watched her as she continued to sing and play. He was surprised that he found her rendition so moving. He was surprised again when he noticed that despite the suit and prim hairdo, Miss Foster was an extremely attractive woman. Even more surprising was the sudden realization that she resembled the woman whom she was imitating so perfectly. Miss Foster had the same wide, almond-shaped cornflower-blue eyes and small, slightly uptilted nose. She had the same high cheekbones, the same wide, sensuous mouth, the same...

Wait a damned minute, he realized suddenly. This *is* Carla Fox. That's why she had seemed so familiar the other day. But why hadn't he recognized her? Admittedly, her hairdo and makeup were different, and she'd been just a teenager when she'd disappeared ten years ago, but still! He'd always been a great fan of Carla Fox. And he'd been wondering for years what had happened to her. Now he knew. She'd become a social worker. Lord, what a laugh! It was funny, really it was, but what a waste of talent! If he could sing half as well as she, he wouldn't be rasping his songs out like an auctioneer on a selling block.

Drake stood a few feet behind and to the side of Carla, and watched as she let her hands fly along the black and white keyboard. The nails of her long, graceful fingers were short and unpolished. A gold watch with a black velvet band was strapped around her narrow wrist.

How could I have thought her cold or unfeeling, he wondered as he listened to her play. The pain and emotion she evoked were so sharp he could feel his insides shattering like glass. How could he have thrown such harsh accusations at her? He remembered them and winced. How could he have condemned her without knowing her? He wasn't usually such a bad judge of character. It was her calm and superior attitude that had fooled him. Obviously the facade was just that.

She wasn't looking calm and superior now. Her blue eyes were bleary, her cheeks streaked with tears. She didn't seem to notice. She was compelled by her music, wrapped up in it.

He felt a strong urge to take her in his arms and comfort her. He knew that she would be soft and yielding to his touch, though not for long. The barriers she kept around herself would soon spring up to protect her. He decided he was going to hold them down as long as possible.

"Damn!" Carla swore suddenly as she made a mistake. She repeated the sequence, but her fingers just weren't quick and sure enough to manage the rapid transition of keys. In a voice choked with tears, she moaned, "I'll never get it right."

Carla dropped her head and let her hands crash on the keyboard. The resounding dissonance was grating, but it was nothing compared to the sound of her heartbroken sobs. Drake felt her agony as if it were his. Without even realizing it, he strode toward her and wrapped her in his arms.

Startled, Carla jumped and pulled back to find Drake watching her with a warm tenderness in his eyes. Where had he come from? she thought with panic. *He knows who I am!* She fought the urge to pull away and flee. She was so tired of playing the coward, so tired of running.

He must know that he had her in the palm of his hand, and that she'd do almost anything to keep her past identity a secret. So why didn't he look superior and triumphant? Why, instead, did his eyes glow warmly as he looked at her?

She shoved an arm between them, trying to break his hold on her. When that failed, she tried rising from the bench, but that was equally useless. He held her fast.

"Be still, I won't hurt you," he whispered, as he pulled her closer. One hand stroked her tangled hair.

The power emanating from him was both fascinating and frightening. He was so overwhelmingly alive and vital. She felt the urge to give in to him, to let his strong arms comfort her. But could she trust him? Especially after what she'd done to him?

Carla raised her head and tried to read an answer in his eyes—and was lost in their compelling depths. Funny, she'd never noticed that his eyes were like amber. Murky and brown, they were spotted with tiny flecks of black.

Carla let out a tired, frustrated cry. There was very little fight left in her. She'd given all her strength and energy to her music, and now, as Drake cradled her in his arms, she felt what remained of her resistance being sapped away.

Drake began to rock back and forth and started singing an old ballad in his harsh, throaty voice. Carla's tightly stretched nerves began to loosen. The words and gentle swaying motion soothed her.

As she leaned against him, she tried to remember the last time someone had sung to her when she'd cried. It had been a very long time. In fact, probably never. She nestled deeper into his arms and sighed with contentment.

The song gently faded out, and Carla lifted her head to find Drake watching her, his rich brown eyes kindly and compassionate. His face was so close that she could see the brown stubble of his beard. Drake smiled tenderly and pulled his head back to look at her from a better angle. "I was always Carla Fox's biggest fan."

"I'm surprised you even remember her," she whispered softly.

"I remember her, all right. I was at your last concert."

Carla's face darkened with the pain of memories. The last concert. That was the day her world had shattered. That was the day the music had died. She felt her hand being squeezed reassuringly.

"Don't be sad," he implored. "You were beautiful that night. And you sang like an angel."

"Never realizing my mother was about to become a *real* angel," she retorted with a bitter look.

"Your mother was never an angel. She was just human like the rest of us. You can't blame yourself for what happened."

"I wish I could believe that," she said wistfully. As an image of her mother falling over the second-story railing to her death came to Carla's mind, she suddenly shuddered and added, "You don't know the whole story. If you did, you would hate me."

"I could never hate you," he assured her softly.

She smiled back at him unbelievingly. "I seem to remember that you weren't too fond of me this morning."

"That's because I didn't know you."

"You still don't," she reminded him, looking steadily into his eyes. "You just think you do. But you don't, believe me."

"Let's not talk about that now," he urged. "Let me sing to you instead."

As he sang, she felt his hand on her back, stroking and comforting her. She felt so close to him, so in tune with his body and his mind. She'd never felt this way with anyone before.

In a low husky voice, he began to croon another song. She felt warm and . . . loving. And from the way his body was melding with hers, she knew he felt the same.

Carla had thought she was drained of all emotion, but this man seemed to stir her hidden resources. She pressed her body into his. She heard the heavy rasping of his breath, smelled the clean male scent of him.

She ran a hand along the back of his neck and felt the downy hairs on his skin bristle.

The urge to touch him, to know him, was powerful. Drake was strong, yet so tender; gentle, but breathtakingly masculine. She wanted him to hold her forever. She wanted him....

Carla lifted her head and looked into Drake's eyes. Then her gaze dropped to his lips as the song faltered and stopped.

Through clouded senses, she heard the creaking of floorboards in the hallway outside and the shuffling of footsteps. The doorknob rattled and she broke away from Drake.

A teenager with shaggy blond hair and more arms and legs than he knew what to do with stuck his head in the door. His freckle-spattered nose and wide, irrepressible grin were deceptively young and innocent: Bobby Dixon had been on the streets since he was six. "Drake! There you are. I've been looking all over for you. Mrs. Rice just told me the good news."

"Oh, hello, Bobby," Drake said in a voice ragged with emotion.

"What's going on?" Bobby gazed from one adult to another with a quizzical, puzzled expression.

"Nothing," Carla broke in. She turned toward the piano to hide her tear-streaked face. In a muffled voice, she added, "Tell me, Bobby, what's the good news?"

The boy shot Drake a knowing look. "Haven't you told her yet?"

Carla wiped the tears from her face with the back of her hand, then turned around and demanded, "Hasn't he told me what?"

Drake ran a hand nervously through his hair, a contrite expression shadowing his face. "That's why I came in here to talk to you. I thought you should know. Mrs. Rice has reversed your decision. She's going to let me adopt Bobby, after all. But until the courts can make everything legal, she's releasing him to my custody as a foster parent, effective tomorrow."

Chapter Three

Carla chewed her bottom lip as she tried to ignore the whine of the fan in the window. Usually she managed to tune out the noise, but not today. Throwing her pen down on the desk in disgust, she got up from her chair and turned the fan off. Silence. Maybe now she could get some work done, Carla thought. If she didn't burn up first. Summer had come early to Los Angeles, and the temperature seemed stuck on broil.

She sat down once again and began to fill out her report, trying to ignore the burning sting of smog in her eyes. Sweat drenched her beige silk suit. It must be the chemical haze that was making it so difficult for her to concentrate, she rationalized. And the heat that was making her feel so dissatisfied with her life. It couldn't be thoughts of Drake Lanning. Oh, no! Certainly not!

She should have been furious with Drake for going to Elizabeth behind her back. Instead she was glad. The decision that had been made three days ago was out of her hands now. If things didn't work out for Bobby, it wouldn't be her fault.

Anyway, it appeared she *had* misjudged Drake. She'd been surprised when Drake, guitar in hand, had showed up this morning. But the real surprise was the van full of guitars that had accompanied him. Drake's three younger brothers, all members of his band, had come, too, promising lessons to anyone who was big enough to hold a guitar.

When one of the younger children had discovered that he was too small to hold a guitar, Drake had merely said, "No problem," and scooped the child into his lap. "I'll hold you and you can play my guitar instead."

Get back to work, Carla reminded herself sternly, pushing away the memory. Don't think of Drake and his laughing brown eyes. Drake is just part of a case that has already been written up and submitted. He's nothing to you; you're nothing to him.

If only she could make herself believe that.

When the phone rang, she grabbed the receiver eagerly, grateful for the distraction. She wouldn't admit, even to herself, that she'd been hoping the caller was Drake. Instead, it was Elizabeth, requesting Carla's presence in her office right away. Carla suppressed a smile. Elizabeth always wanted things done right away.

The orphanage was located in an old frame house that should have been torn down years ago. The plumbing was ancient, and the roof needed reshingling. The basement leaked when it rained. Even if they had the money to repair the building, it hardly seemed worth the expense; something else would just break down.

Carla left her office and passed through the vestibule leading to Elizabeth's office. The vestibule, like the rest of the house, was depressingly in need of redecoration. The walls were covered with faded and torn flowered wallpaper in a vile shade of olive green. The ceiling needed replastering, and the hallway was poorly lit. A scarred mahogany banister led to the second floor.

Carla passed all of this without a glance. These were old and much-complained-about grievances, and it did her no good to notice them. Elizabeth had been pleading with local agencies for new housing for years, but all she ever got was promises and no action.

"Come in and sit down," Elizabeth said as Carla entered the room. Carla had once heard someone describe Elizabeth as having the heart of Florence Nightingale and the mind of Machiavelli. She thought this description very close to the truth. Elizabeth was a stocky woman with faded gray hair that matched her faded gray eyes. There was nothing faded about her personality, however. She was all energy, all action, and always impatient. Elizabeth smiled amiably and motioned for Carla to sit down. "I wanted to talk to you about the Bobby Dixon case."

Carla nodded and took a seat, noting that there was something about Elizabeth that was different today. There was a sense of excitement, of anticipation—and of guarded uneasiness. Carla watched Elizabeth lean back in her chair and smile again. Suddenly it occurred to her. She was getting Elizabeth's public smile, the smile she used for board members and prospective parents. And yet Elizabeth and Carla had been friends for years.

Elizabeth smiled again and said, "I hope you weren't angry that I reversed your decision." Drumming a pencil on her desk, she continued, "I realize you didn't want to do the interview, and that may have colored your thinking. I had hoped that you would be able to view Drake Lanning more objectively."

"It's okay," Carla said. "You were right. I was being overprotective of Bobby. I hated growing up in the public eye. I guess I let my own feelings on the subject color my judgment."

"Good. I'm glad you see it that way." Elizabeth beamed.

"And?" Carla prodded suspiciously, thinking that something was definitely rotten in the state of California. This wasn't the first time Elizabeth had countermanded one of her recommendations. But it was the first time Elizabeth had called her into her office to discuss the matter.

"And?" Elizabeth repeated with innocent gray eyes. Carla was positive Elizabeth hadn't looked that innocent since kindergarten.

Carla sighed. "We've known each other too long to start playing cat and mouse now. Either tell me what you've got on your mind or let me get back to work."

Elizabeth hesitated, tapping her pencil against the desk again. "Mr. Lanning called today…"

"I don't like the sound of it already, but go on."

Elizabeth stood and walked over to the window. Her figure filled out completely the capacious blue-flowered tent dress she wore. At last she said, "Mr. Lanning has offered to do a rock concert with all proceeds to go to the orphanage."

"That's wonderful!" Carla exclaimed.

"Unfortunately there's a catch," Elizabeth interrupted briskly. "Mr. Lanning refuses to do the concert unless you agree to perform with him onstage."

For a moment it sounded glorious. Imagine being on the stage again, Carla thought, singing in front of a crowd. She heard the sound of instruments tuning up. She felt the excitement…the tension…the spotlights on a darkened platform. And then the hush as she and Drake stepped forward.

But then she pictured her mother, the famous and sometimes infamous Gloria Styles in the royal-blue gown she'd worn at their last concert. She saw her mother and herself coming home that evening and climbing the stairs to their bedrooms as the telephone began to ring. Her mother had laughingly answered the phone, but her laughter had soon turned to violent anger.

Carla closed her eyes to squeeze back the tears. That nightmare of an evening had occurred over ten years ago, but it would never be over for her. All she needed was to make one careless slip of the tongue and she would wind up in jail for life. Worse still, she would ruin the career and the life of someone who had lied to protect her.

"I can't do it," Carla managed, visibly shaken. Her voice became stronger. "After all, I haven't performed in years. The whole idea's ridiculous."

"I tried to explain that to him," Elizabeth said, waddling slowly back to her chair. "But he wouldn't listen."

"But why would he suggest such a thing?" Carla demanded, cocking her head to the side. "He doesn't need me to help sell tickets. All he has to do is grind his hips."

"I told him it was impossible," Elizabeth remarked, lifting her hands in helplessness. "I told him you'd never consider it. That ever since your mother died you've been afraid to perform."

Carla groaned. "You didn't tell him that!"

Elizabeth eased herself back in her chair. "Why, yes, I did. It's the truth, isn't it?"

"Of course it's not the truth," Carla retorted. "I'm not one bit afraid."

"Then what are you?"

"Wise." Carla shifted the glasses on her nose and moistened her lips with her tongue. "I cherish my pri-

vacy. You don't know what I've been through. You
don't know what it was like—the reporters, the cameras, the gawking crowds of fans. Do you have any
idea of the publicity this one little performance would
bring?''

"I know," Elizabeth agreed with a sigh. "But it's
only for one night. And we need that money so desperately."

*Only for one night. It might as well be for an eter-
nity.* Carla felt the blast of tears start to come. Rising
quickly, she crossed to the window. Through her tears
she watched the children playing baseball on the grass.
Her heart went out to them. They were orphans, just
like her. Many of them had been physically abused,
just like her. But unlike her, they were small and help-
less. They didn't yet know how to cope with the harsh
realities of life. She'd do almost anything to help and
protect them.

Anything but this, she told herself fiercely. She'd
become a social worker to help abused children, but
asking her to do this concert was asking too much.
Everyone had their limits, and this was hers.

"I know the concert's for only one night," Carla
explained in a quiet voice. "But that one night would
disrupt my life. It's taken years for people to forget
Gloria Styles and Carla Fox. The only reason people
have is because I disappeared. My reappearance would
bring it all back. The press would have a holiday.
They'd dredge up every horrible detail of my mother's death.'' Her voice cracked and she paused before

she continued, "I can't go through that again. I'm not strong enough. Please don't ask me."

Carla heard the squeak of Elizabeth's chair as it swiveled around. "Carla..." Elizabeth's voice was gentle.

"Yes?" came the muffled reply.

"Please turn around and accept this tissue."

Carla turned around and took the tissue. "Thanks."

Elizabeth rolled her chair over to Carla, grabbed her hand and gave it a squeeze. Her chair squeaked as she leaned forward and said, "Carla, you're so strong. You've got so much to give. Your only problem is yourself. If you could just learn to get over your fears you'd be a much happier person."

"I am happy," Carla responded hoarsely.

"Then why are you crying?" Elizabeth asked gently.

"Because I'm remembering the past."

"When you learn to conquer your fear of the past you won't have to cry about it anymore."

"I'm not afraid," Carla wailed. For a moment she considered telling Elizabeth what had really happened the night her mother died. If she told her, Elizabeth would understand why she couldn't stand being in the limelight. But she couldn't do it. She'd kept her painful feelings and thoughts buried for years, and to talk about them might be like opening Pandora's box. It wasn't just her secret to tell, anyway; it was Dr. Cook's secret, too. Summoning up all her self-control, she said evenly, "I'm also not a masochist. What you're asking of me is too much—" She hesitated, looking for a tactful way to say what she was thinking. "What you're asking is too much of an imposition."

"You're right," Elizabeth said wearily as she handed Carla another tissue. "It is too much of an imposition. Let's talk about something else. Like how we're going to get the money to pay for Cliff Richard's operation. Or how we're going to get the money for a new building!" She stopped for a second and seemed to ponder. "I know! We could have another car wash. That always brings in fifty or a hundred dollars—"

"Elizabeth!" Carla cried, jerking her hand away. Now she understood Elizabeth's game strategy. Elizabeth knew that shouting and begging would never work, but challenging her—playing on her fears—might.

"Think it over, my dear," Elizabeth said. This time Carla got the benefit of her private smile. "You know I wouldn't want to put any undue pressure on you."

"In a pig's eye you wouldn't want to put any undue pressure on me," Carla spat out her words. Stalking toward the door, she pivoted and stopped. "It was a good performance, but not quite good enough. I'm on to you, Elizabeth. And you're not going to challenge me or shame me into performing. My answer is no and it will always be no." Carla stuck her hands on her hips and regarded Elizabeth defiantly. Her eyes blazed like burning blue coals. "How can you even think of pressuring me into doing this? You, of all people! You're the one who helped me get back on my feet. You're the one who first suggested I change my name and disguise my appearance.''

"I know, I know. But I've been wondering for years if I gave you bad advice," Elizabeth said with a weary sigh. "Carla, you'll never be a whole person, you'll never have a moment's peace until you face who and what you are." She inched her chair back to her desk and folded her hands on the desktop. "Don't get me wrong. I'm not criticizing your work—you do a good job. You do an excellent job. You really care about the children and you understand them. You've been on the receiving end of the same kind of mental and physical abuse they've endured. But it's time that you faced up to facts. You're a fine social worker; you're a great musician. And now it's time for you to quit blaming music and yourself for what happened. Why do you insist on shunning music when it once brought you such joy?''

Carla's laugh was bitter. "Hasn't it occurred to you that I might fall flat on my cute little derriere? I haven't sung in years, and Drake's style isn't exactly compatible with mine.''

"That's more like it," Elizabeth said smugly. "Now you're being honest with yourself. I told you that you were afraid.''

"I'm not afraid!" Carla denied hotly.

"Then prove it. Go and sing your heart out with that gorgeous hunk. And while you're at it, give him a great big kiss for me." Elizabeth gave Carla a glance that looked surprisingly like a leer. "If I were thirty years younger and fifty pounds lighter I'd jump at the chance to get near Drake Lanning." She smiled placidly, steepled her fingers and added, "Or are you afraid of him, too?"

Carla turned on her heel and marched back into her own office. After slamming the door shut, she admitted the truth to herself. She *was* afraid.

Later that afternoon Carla screeched out of the parking lot like a race-car driver. She thought about going home, but decided to stop at her favorite burrito stand first. The stand, a ramshackle hole-in-the-wall, advertised itself as having the largest, sloppiest and spiciest burritos in all of California. Carla ordered three burritos, one more than her normal quota, deciding that if she were going to go down, she'd go down fighting . . . and fat. Requesting the burritos for takeout, she grabbed the neatly wrapped bag and headed for her car.

Carla zipped out of the parking lot. The orphanage and the burrito stand were in Pasadena, while Carla's home was located in the winding hills of Eagle Rock, a small community adjacent to Pasadena. She crossed busy Colorado Boulevard, famous for the New Year's Day Rose Bowl Parade, then wheeled the car onto the bridge that spanned the dry riverbed of the Arroyo Grande. The car's tires made a hollow, thumping sound as it traversed the bridge. On solid ground again, she turned the car to the right, then shoved the stick forward and let it labor up the steep hill to her home.

Carla loved her house. She'd lived in it five years, which was a record for her. Owning a place that she could call her own was a luxury for her—one that many people took for granted.

The neighborhood she lived in was stable, middle-class and unpretentious. People paid as much attention to their lawns as they did to their neighbors' private lives. Carla waved to several neighbors as she passed by. Middle America was right here in Eagle Rock, California, and she loved it. But she couldn't help wondering what these respectable, conservative people would think if they discovered that she was Carla Fox.

Carla Fox died ten years ago, she reminded herself sternly. The idea of her being resurrected was preposterous. What was on Drake's mind to propose such a ridiculous idea? What was in it for him? He wouldn't have suggested such an idea without reasons.

But what were his reasons? Beneath the casual arrogance, she knew there had to be some good in him, otherwise he wouldn't be so interested in helping Bobby Dixon. Was he trying to help her too, she wondered? But why should he bother? Why should he even care? More to the point—why did he consider it was any of his darned business?

Carla reached her house, an unassuming little bungalow perched on top of the hill. It looked out on a valley congested with buildings and roads and a house-studded ridge of hills. Sometimes she had a marvelous view, but today all she could see was the gray, cloying gloom of Los Angeles smog. Luckily it didn't matter. She wasn't in the mood to admire the view anyway.

Carla parked her car in the driveway and grabbed her bag of burritos. Her tan wire-haired terrier, Lady Catherine de Bourgh, named after one of Carla's favorite Jane Austen characters, was waiting at the door for her as she opened the front door. Giving Lady Catherine a pat on the head, she said, "Yes, poochkins, I brought you a burrito. But you're going to have to wait for a few minutes."

The house was stifling from being closed up all day. Walking over to the room thermostat, she set the temperature for sixty degrees, thinking that perhaps a cool room would cool her temper.

As she walked toward the kitchen, she peeled off various items of clothing. The image she projected of compulsive neatness was just that—an image. Carla was a slob at heart. Growing up with a neurotically neat mother had made her rebel against being tidy, and had propelled her toward a life of chronic chaos.

The eyeglasses and the bobby pins that held up her hair landed on top of the television. Her jacket she tossed on the couch, her blouse on the coffee table. Stopping in the entranceway to the kitchen, she leaned against the door frame and peeled off her panty hose. She tossed them toward the top of the refrigerator and watched them land against the side and slither to the nearby kitchen table. She wrinkled her nose in distaste, but left them there anyway.

By the time she was pouring herself a tall glass of rum and Coke, she had stripped to her bikini panties and bra. She was still hot, but at least she was free of the confines of clothing.

Lady Catherine had followed Carla's pilgrimage to the kitchen. She knew the familiar smell of burritos at fifty paces. Carla pulled a burrito from the bag and undid its white wax-paper wrapping. Ripping off several large, dripping hunks, she told Lady Catherine, "Here you go. Pig out. And I hope you get indigestion. I asked for extra-hot sauce."

Carla sat down on a chair at the kitchen table and propped her feet up on the opposite chair. Unwrapping a burrito, she took a large bite. As she chewed, she tried to decide who she was the maddest at. Probably Drake, she decided, as she felt sour cream, hot sauce and beans ooze down her arm. She searched through the white paper bag, found a couple of napkins and wiped her arm clean. Yes, definitely, she decided, taking another bite. If he hadn't called Elizabeth with his ridiculous demands for a concert, the whole thing wouldn't have happened.

How could he do this to me? she thought resentfully. What colossal nerve! She pulled off a piece of burrito and fed it to the dog, who wagged her tail in thanks. Doesn't he realize that part of my life is finished? she asked herself. That I have no interest in ever performing again?

If only it were true, she reflected dolefully. If it were, then she would do this one concert and be done with it. But she was afraid that music to her was like a drink to an alcoholic. One concert might set her back on the road to self-destruction. Her performance at the piano the other day had showed her the danger signs.

Elizabeth was right: she was afraid. The prospect of this concert was tempting, but... If only she didn't have to deal with the publicity, she might be able to handle it. If only she didn't have to worry about the secrets from her past being exposed. She was too innately honest to lie to herself. She still loved music. She missed music. She hadn't realized how badly she'd missed it until the other day.

She finished one burrito and started another, assuring herself she liked her life the way it was. It was calm. It was predictable. It might be a trifle boring, but so what? It was better than the frenetic roller coaster of her youth, right?

Gulping down the last of her burrito, she took a long sip of her drink and reflected. If she needed a change it was her business and no one else's. It was true that she'd been feeling a trifle dissatisfied with her life lately. She'd begun to feel as though her life were a fast-paced freeway with no on or off ramps, and no pleasant excursions in between. All she did was rush, rush, rush, but she never seemed to get anywhere.

Still, that didn't give Elizabeth and Drake the right to interfere with her life. Whatever happened was her own decision. She didn't tell them what to do. What gave them the right to tell her?

If only Drake were here, she thought resentfully. She'd give him a piece of her mind. How dare he put pressure on her? How dare he make her out to be the villain of this melodrama?

She picked up the remains of the last burrito. Maybe if she ate herself silly, Drake wouldn't want to be seen with her onstage.

She took another bite. She had a lot of eating to do in the next month if she were going to get that fat. But even as she felt the crunch of the lettuce and flour tortilla beneath her teeth, she knew it wouldn't work; she had a metabolism as quick as a hummingbird's. Every time she'd gone on a diet to gain weight, she wound up losing instead.

Life was sometimes very unfair.

Drake sat in the shade of his patio strumming music on his old Gibson guitar. He always used the Gibson when he was composing music; he liked its soft sounds and the memories of his youth. The Gibson was the first decent guitar he'd ever owned, bought with money he'd made at the age of fifteen, working as a busboy after school.

He couldn't help feeling surprised at how well Elizabeth had responded to his ultimatum. She'd actually sounded glad when he'd told her that he wouldn't do the performance without Carla. Resorting to blackmail wasn't something he liked to do, but it was the only way he could think of to make Carla do this concert with him. He wasn't really sure why he was so determined. As a teenager he'd had a crush on Carla Fox that had just faded away when she'd disappeared from the scene. Now, seeing her again revived all the feelings he'd had for her as a love-struck kid. Only now he knew her, and he was a man...

He picked a song out on his guitar. It was a sad, lonely love song, one he'd written the other night in honor of Carla. It told the story of a man in love with a woman he'd never met.

Maybe I am still a little infatuated with her, he thought wryly, strumming his fingers across the guitar strings.

Funny that he hadn't recognized her right away. There was a time in his life when he'd seen nothing but Carla Fox's face. He remembered Carla and her mother's last concert. At the time he'd been an insignificant guitarist playing in an even more insignificant nightclub. He'd worked extra nights for a month to save the money to treat his family and himself to that evening.

His parents had been ardent Gloria Styles and Carla Fox movie fans. He could still picture his parents piling everyone into the family car—an old blue Rambler station wagon with more rattles than a diamondback—and heading for the local drive-in to see the latest Styles/Fox movie. Growing up, Drake had always admired Carla in her movies, but at eighteen, when he'd seen her in concert, he'd been enchanted. He hadn't been able to get her out of his mind. She was so sad, so vulnerable, and yet so alive and sensual. The memory of her had haunted him for months.

He remembered the morning after the concert when the newspapers had announced her mother's mysterious and tragic death. They'd sold all their papers that day. Later, the coroner's office disclosed that Gloria had slipped on a rug and fallen over the second-story railing in her house. Carla's doctor had ordered her into immediate seclusion.

Drake had felt the whole thing intensely, as if it had happened to himself or someone dear to him. For several months afterward, the newspapers were full of news of Carla Fox. How she'd been unable to attend her mother's funeral and had been committed to a sanitarium for rest. He'd read everything he could get his hands on about her. Some of the news was true, some exaggerated, some obvious fiction. Then one day Carla had disappeared . . . drifted out of the news and out of his life.

He'd dreamed that he'd get to know Carla Fox better, when her pain had healed. Later was now, but he wasn't at all sure the pain had healed.

Not that he blamed her. She hadn't had it easy growing up. She'd been performing with her mother in movies by the age of three. Had she ever had a chance to be a kid? To do kid things? Drake thought of his middle-class family and the home life they'd given him. There had never been money for extras, but there had always been plenty of love and stability.

He knew from the magazine articles he'd devoured when he was younger that Carla's care had consisted mainly of nannies and governesses. Her father, movie director Daniel Fox, had been killed in a plane crash before Carla was born.

No, Carla hadn't had it easy growing up, Drake decided. And here he was playing games with her; putting pressure on her to perform again. He twanged his fingers noisily across the guitar strings. Remembering the agony he'd put her through the other day, he felt even worse. He didn't know why he was doing this to her, but he knew that for some reason he had to. There was something in her that called out to him, that wanted to be set free, even as Carla fought against it. If only he could explain this to her, maybe then she would understand. If only he could talk to her...

Instinct and emotion came to the fore. Springing up from his chair, he walked across the patio and opened the French door with a twist of its brass handle. Entering the room, he made his way to the telephone and dialed.

"Hello, Elizabeth?" he demanded when he'd been connected. "I know it's a big favor to ask, but would you mind giving me Carla's address? I know she's probably mad enough to put a contract out on my murder, but I thought maybe if I explained things she'd forgive me. Yes, I know you're not supposed to give out such information, but please, anyway?"

He scrambled for a pen, grateful that one of his maid's duties was to make sure the telephone stand was supplied with paper and pen. He shifted the receiver in his hand and asked, "Now, what was that again? Yes, I've got it. And thanks."

Chapter Four

Carla was lounging on the couch with the air conditioner blasting wafts of cold air all over her body, which was resplendent in lace-trimmed lavender bikini panties and a matching lavender lace bra. A glass filled with rum and Coke was in her right hand as she tried to watch her favorite evening newscaster. Usually the wry smile and warm, sexy brown eyes of the announcer on TV managed to keep her mind on the screen—and sometimes even on the topic being discussed.

Tonight was an exception. Tonight she couldn't help seeing another pair of brown eyes, so warm that they resembled molten amber. She also saw Drake's impudent grin, his flash of sparkling white teeth, and the

habit he had of flicking his curly brown hair out of his
face with a hand.

Setting her glass down on the coffee table, she
crossed one long, slim leg over the other and tried to
concentrate on listening to the news. Her fingers
tapped restlessly against the side of the couch. The
situation in Central America was tense, but not nearly
as tense as she was feeling at the moment. Damn
Drake Lanning, she thought, picking up her glass and
taking a long swallow of rum and Coke. What gave
him the right to treat her like a pawn on a chess-
board?

When the melodic chimes of her doorbell sounded,
she wondered if she should bother to get up to answer
it. People rarely dropped by to see her. Only her
neighbor Sheila, spacey, fun-loving Sheila, came un-
announced to her door. Otherwise it was usually just
someone trying to sell her something.

Still, it would be nice to have someone to talk to,
even if it was just Sheila coming over to gripe about
the latest peccadilloes of her ex-husband. And hearing about another man's faults might cheer her up.
Carla knew she was much too keyed up to concentrate on anything else tonight.

Spotting her favorite red silk kimono crumpled on
the floor behind a bentwood rocker, Carla stooped
over and picked it up. As she pulled the kimono over
her shoulders, she said a prayer of thanks that the
wrinkled look was in.

She almost didn't open the door when she peeked
through the peephole and saw who was standing out-

side on the front door stoop: Drake Lanning. He looked tall and gorgeous and very male. He was just who she wanted—if she were armed.

As her fingers unfastened the chain lock, she wondered how Drake had gotten her address. It wasn't listed in the telephone book. Had Elizabeth given it to him? That seemed the most likely answer, she decided, thinning her lips into a tight line.

"Good evening," Drake greeted with a small bow as the door swung open. The rugged, sharply chiseled lines of his tanned face were fixed in a polite but wary smile.

"You! Of all the nerve," Carla replied. Her blue eyes were frosty and narrowed. "I won't ask why you're here. I already know. But I will ask you this: What gives you the right to interfere with my life?"

"I knew you'd be upset," Drake replied, his eyes on the kimono, where it clung to her breasts. He approved, she could tell from the gleam in his eyes and the way he lifted a dark eyebrow. "That's why I'm here. May I come in?"

"The bug man came last week," Carla said, refusing to budge from the door. "I thought he'd exterminated all the pests in my life, but I guess he must have missed one. A big one."

"Funny, very funny," Drake said calmly, leaning an arm against the doorjamb. "Now you'd better let me in before I start causing a scene. I can sing pretty loudly when I have to, and your neighbors look pretty interested in what's going on here."

Scowling, she stepped aside to let him enter. Drake entered the room with a lithe, athletic grace. On any other man, the red, beige and black flowered silk Hawaiian shirt he was wearing would have appeared effeminate. On him it looked bold and aggressively masculine, emphasizing the aura of raw, virile sexuality he exuded. The colorful shirt fell loosely over beige linen tweed pants that hugged his narrow hips and emphasized his long, powerfully muscled legs.

In a defensive gesture, Carla wrapped the front lapels of her kimono tightly over her breasts, unaware that she was delineating even further the voluptuous splendor of her body. "I'd offer you something to drink, but I know this isn't a social call. And I like to save the good stuff for pleasant company."

"That's okay," Drake replied with mocking eyes, "I don't like to ruin the silken cords with the hard stuff, anyway."

"You could have fooled me," Carla retorted. "I thought your vocal cords must be lined with gravel. How else do you manage to sound so hoarse?"

Drake grinned but made no response as his eyes took in the room. Noticing the chaos, he lifted an inquisitive eyebrow and asked, "What happened? Was it Hurricane Alice or Earthquake Carla?"

"Tell me, Mr. Lanning," Carla said, determined not to let him know she was embarrassed by her disreputable housekeeping, "to what do I owe this great displeasure?"

Drake flashed a knowing grin at her as he leaned over and picked up a pair of white nylon shorts lying on a chair. As he tossed them on top of a pile of newspapers, he sat down on the chair. "I've come here to discuss the concert we'll be doing together."

"I'd rather freeze in hell than do a concert with you," Carla retorted. Shoving a pile of paperback books to the far corner of the couch, she plunked herself down. "But since you're here to talk, we'll talk. Explain to me your motivation. Explain to me why you told Elizabeth one of the conditions was that I perform."

"The answer's quite simple," Drake replied, stretching his long legs in front of him. "I want to do a concert with you."

"The whole idea's preposterous!" Carla scoffed, tossing her head. "Why, I haven't performed in ages. That part of my life is finished."

"And why is it finished?" he countered. The tension in Drake's voice made Carla look up quickly. His eyes had that dangerous look that was becoming all too familiar to her. He went on, "I'll tell you why: because you don't have the guts to climb back on that stage and face what you really are."

"I know what I am," Carla replied sharply, springing up and pacing the room. She turned and looked at him, a frown creasing the space between her eyes. "I'm a social worker, not a singer."

Sitting up, Drake crossed one leg over the other and tried to remain calm as he reasoned with her. "Look, Carla, a voice like yours is a gift. I know plenty of singers who would sell their souls to sing like you do.

You have no right to hide away just because life got a little too tough."

Carla jutted her chin and said, "I'm not hiding away. I'm just trying to do something constructive with my life."

His lips twisted into a mocking smile. "Okay, then, let's see you put your money where your mouth is. If you really mean what you say, you'll do this concert. I'll guarantee the orphanage half a million dollars clear. If we don't make that much out of the proceeds, I'll pay the rest out of my own pocket."

"That's blackmail!" Carla protested, beginning to pace even faster. She came to an abrupt halt at the end of the room and shoved the curtain at the window aside. Half a million dollars! They could buy and furnish a mansion and still have money left over. Had Drake promised Elizabeth that much? If he had, it was no wonder she'd been so excited.

"Yes, it's blackmail," he conceded. "But think of all that lovely money. Think of the good you could do. And most of all, think of how guilty you're going to feel when you look at those kids and remember that you had it in your power to make their lives better."

"Why are you doing this?" Carla demanded furiously. She blinked her eyes, trying to blot out tears. She turned and looked at him and, in a voice breaking with emotion, asked, "Do you enjoy torturing me? Is this your way of getting even?"

Drake saw the fear and hurt spilling from her blue eyes. He didn't understand it, but he knew it was there. He didn't like feeling responsible for it, but he'd gone too far to turn back now. Promising himself that one day he'd make it up to her, he replied blandly, "Why should I want to get even?"

"Why?" she retorted, her voice catching on a sob. "Because I turned down your application to adopt Bobby, that's why."

"Oh, that—" Drake waved a hand "—that was no big deal. After all, I did win out eventually."

"Is winning so very important?" Carla asked softly. "Is it worth half a million dollars to make me look like a fool?"

"That's not what this is all about," Drake replied. He stood and in two long strides he was next to her and pulling her into his arms. As he twisted her around to face him, he felt her body tremble, saw the traces of tears across her pale face. She was so vulnerable, so slender and small. Although she tried to appear tough, he wasn't fooled.

There was a mystery about her, an elusive quality that fascinated him. Perhaps that was why he felt so compelled to do this concert with her. Stroking the tears from her face, he said gently, "I was always a big fan of yours. I used to dream about playing a concert with you. I guess you could say this is my chance to fulfill a lifetime dream."

"Dreams are something only fools believe in," Carla said with a sob.

"Not this one." His fingers weaved through the long blond silk of her hair.

"Why? What makes you so sure? You hardly know me," Carla answered, trying to break away. His brown eyes studied her intently, belying the gentle hold of his arms.

"I know you better than you know yourself," he contended.

"You don't know me at all," Carla replied quickly. "You just think you do."

"Oh, yes, I know you. And I'll show you," he said, as his lips gently covered hers.

He was right. He did know her...in the most important way between a man and a woman. As she felt his breath against her neck, she slid her hands along the silky softness of his shirt, reveling in the feel of the tightly corded muscles of his back. He was so warm and alive; so intense. She'd never known such strength and vitality in a man before.

She heard him moan—whether in pleasure or agony, she couldn't tell. She tilted her head back to see.

Up close, she noticed the rough texture of his skin as it stretched across the angular jut of his cheekbones and nose. Dark stubble surrounded his mouth with the growth of half a day's beard. His smell was woodsy and overpoweringly male.

Her breathing seemed to stop when she saw his eyes. Their rich brown color glowed like amber. Desire and barely leashed control shone through, and she knew that they reflected what was probably evident in her own eyes.

"You asked me why I didn't want to do this concert with you," she managed to say at last, a bit breathlessly. Her nerves were screeching like a burglar alarm out of control. The analogy reminded her of her imminent peril and destruction. He could rob her of everything she held dear—her privacy, her freedom, her self-respect, even her sanity. She added, "You've just demonstrated to me another reason."

"Why?" he demanded. "Because I want to make love to you?"

"Because you want to go to bed with me," she corrected. "I doubt that love is involved at all."

"You don't know how I feel for you," he parried, stroking the tangle of hair away from her face. "I might be madly in love with you."

"I doubt it," Carla refuted sharply. "Love doesn't strike that quickly."

"But I've really known you for years," he said with a teasing smile. "I will admit you need a chance to get to know me better. Would you agree to do this concert if I promised to behave? To keep my hands to myself . . . unless I'm invited?"

"Is that possible?" Carla asked, looking deep into his eyes. "You strike me as a man with a strong—" she hesitated as she searched for a suitable euphemism "—you strike me as a man with a strong libido."

"I never let my libido out in public unless it's on a strong leash," he assured her, his brown eyes twinkling. "I promise not to touch you unless you invite me. How's that for a deal?"

"I still don't understand," Carla replied, shaking her head. "Why do you want to sing with me? You heard me the other day. I sounded as bad as a cracked Stradivarius."

"We can change that," Drake said, stepping away from her. "You'd be surprised what a few weeks of practice can do."

"I would be surprised," Carla said dryly, pulling her hands away from him. "Anyway, I've never sung rock before. I doubt I could handle it."

"You'll never know until you try. Do you want it on your conscience that you were too much of a coward to even try?"

She flinched at his words and turned away from him as he said softly, "Trust me, Carla. I promise I won't betray you. I wouldn't be offering you this absurd challenge if I didn't think it would work."

His admitting his challenge was absurd rattled her. If only it wasn't *him*. If only she didn't find him so attractive. If only, if only... Carla bit her bottom lip nervously and admitted, "I wouldn't mind doing this concert so much if it weren't for the publicity. The thought of all those people hounding me again terrifies me."

"Is that all you're worried about? We can get around that. What if I promise you complete anonymity? You show up for this one concert as Carla Fox and then poof! You disappear again."

Carla wrinkled her brow as she thought about this. "Would that be possible—for me to disappear again?"

"I don't see why not. After all, this is only one concert. Of course, we'll have to keep the location of our practice sessions a secret, but that's no big deal. We're old hands at that."

The offer sounded tempting. She was too honest to deny it. She said hesitantly, "I'd do it if it just wasn't rock. Rock's not my style." As soon as the words came out, Carla realized what she was doing; she was beginning to give in.

"Snob," he accused with an ironic lift of his dark eyebrows.

"I am not," Carla protested. "I like rock. I listen to it all the time. It's just that I've never sung it before."

"There's always a first time. Anyway, the songs I've been writing lately aren't really rock at all. They're more 'torch' rhythm-and-blues kind of stuff. Would you like to hear one?"

Carla looked doubtful. With a gleam in his eyes, Drake suggested, "Oh, come on, listening to one song won't kill you."

"Okay. Just one song," she conceded. What harm could listening to one song do?

"I'll be right back," he promised. "Let me go get my guitar. It's in the car."

"I see you came prepared," she said dryly as he reentered the house, his battered Gibson guitar tucked under his arm.

He grinned unabashedly and said, "At least I didn't bring it into the house initially. Give me credit for some tact." Sprawling out on a chair, he began to tune his guitar.

"I think that was craftiness, not tact," Carla retorted.

He flashed her a guilty, mischievous smile. Then he began to sing. His voice was low and throaty and rich. And very, very seductive. Carla watched as his long tapered fingers plucked knowingly over the guitar strings. She liked the easy, expert way he touched them. But it was his words that captivated her. It was his words that touched her. He had barely begun the second refrain before Carla suddenly realized that his song, "The Lady with Tears," was about her.

Carla's eyes were misting when he finished. In a voice that cracked as she spoke, Carla said, "That was a beautiful song. But I could never sing it in public. It's too personal. It's too moving. I'm afraid I'd break down in front of the audience."

"You'll sing it," he said confidently. "The really good songs always hurt when you sing them." Noticing the incredulous look on her face, he added, "You don't believe me? It's true. Think about it for a moment. Anything that's really good comes from suffering. Did you ever see any of Van Gogh's work? Have you ever read Tolstoy? They were both unhappy, driven men. That's what made them great."

"You don't strike me as an unhappy, driven man," Carla said, remembering the normal, stable life he'd led as a child. It was so different from the life she'd known as a child. She added, "It doesn't seem to me that you've had to endure too much suffering."

"No one's life is ever as easy as it appears on the surface," Drake countered. "Including mine."

"You think so?" Carla asked, her blue eyes regarding him thoughtfully. "It seems to me you've got everything most people want—money, fame."

"Money and fame are a bore," Drake said with a wave of a hand. He looked at her keenly. "You should know that. You've had them. Sure, they're nice; sure, they make you feel important and comfortable. But I could live without them. I wouldn't be heartbroken if I lost them all tomorrow."

"Is there anything you would be heartbroken about if you lost it tomorrow?" Carla queried, at the same time asking herself the same question. She didn't like the answer she came up with.

Drake's hand strummed the guitar as he replied, "Lots of things would leave me heartbroken—losing my family, losing my friends, losing my self-respect. I don't really give a hoot 'n' holler what the rest of the world thinks of me. All I care about is what I think of me. And the people in my life come first."

A feeling of emptiness assailed Carla. The only person in her life who came first was Elizabeth. Carla couldn't imagine having a whole family to care about. It must be wonderful—and a great responsibility. Obviously, Drake took that responsibility very seriously.

"Do you remember Tyler Gunther?" Drake asked suddenly. His fingers twanged nervously across the guitar as his eyes studied the white ceiling.

"Yes, of course," Carla replied. Drake might as well have asked her if she remembered the Beatles. Tyler Gunther had been a popular folk musician who had died a slow and debilitating death from multiple sclerosis a few years before.

Drake stared into the distance. His voice sounded far away when he continued. "Tyler was a buddy of mine. A special buddy, in fact." He looked at Carla and smiled softly. "Remember that car I supposedly stole when I was sixteen? It belonged to Tyler. Instead of pressing charges, Tyler made a deal with me: as long as I stayed in school and kept my grades up, he'd let me play in his band."

"So that's why you were so determined to help Bobby," Carla said with a start of sudden realization.

"Right. Tyler and I stayed friends to the end—and believe me, watching him die was no Rose Bowl Parade."

The pained comment reminded Carla that there was more to Drake than met the eye. Layers. That's what this man was made of, she decided. Every time she pulled away one layer, there was another underneath, just as complicated and just as intriguing. What would happen when she got to the core? Would she be disillusioned? Or more enchanted? Or lost forever?

"I appreciate your telling me about all this," Carla said, reminding herself to keep her guard up. Drake had a way of getting under her skin that spelled danger for her. "I guess your life hasn't been easy. But if you're looking for someone to show hurt and anger on the stage, you've come to the wrong person. I cling to my privacy. I need my privacy. I have no intention of baring my soul in front of an audience for you or anyone."

"I'm not asking you to bare your soul. I'm just asking you to feel my songs. A good voice is dynamite, but it's the emotion you put into the song that matters. That emotion is what once made your singing so great."

"Emotion can be exhausting—and very painful," Carla said bitterly.

"Emotion can be a release—and a catharsis." He strummed his fingers across the guitar. "Why don't we listen to another song I've written for our concert?"

"I don't remember agreeing to do the concert," Carla objected.

"You did. Not in so many words, maybe," he admitted, smiling. "But you know you want to do it."

She couldn't deny it. "Okay. Sing me one more song."

So he did. The song was a sad, wistful ballad about a man in love with a woman who didn't even know he existed. Once again, his poetry captivated her. Once again, his music intoxicated her.

And there was more. After finishing this song, Drake started on another. Carla felt frustration beginning to build in her. She could never be passive when it came to music. That was the reason she'd shunned music for so many years. If she was near it, she had to be part of it; she had to perform.

Fleetingly, she thought that she hadn't taken the first drink yet; but she was looking down the road of a good long binge.

Drake, noting the play of emotion on Carla's face, felt both pleasure and guilt. He knew he had hooked her. She wouldn't be able to say no now. But was he doing the right thing? Would this help her? Or was he simply being selfish, trying to satisfy his own needs? He couldn't say, for sure.

When Drake finished, he said, "Why don't you help me with the next one? I have the two-part harmony all worked out."

"Yes, why not," Carla said. Suddenly she felt reckless and eager and alive—alive for the first time in years.

The song wasn't anything like her old style. It was much faster, much jazzier. But it suited her voice anyway. Best of all, it was fun to sing. As she sang the high notes and Drake sang the low, she couldn't help wondering how they would sound on tape. She thought their voices complemented one another nicely, but one never really knew until you ran the tape....

"You wouldn't happen to have a tape recorder," Drake asked, seeming to read her mind. "I'd sure like to hear how we sound."

"I have a cassette player. It's not a fine piece of sound equipment..."

"But it's better than nothing," Drake finished. "Bring it out and let's see what happens."

She disappeared into the bedroom and returned with a small cassette recorder in one hand and a microphone with a badly tangled cord in the other. She plugged the machine in and set it to record. Drake began strumming his guitar and, after taking a deep breath, Carla began the song.

A few minutes later they stopped and played back what they had just done.

"I told you we'd sound great together!" Drake exclaimed exuberantly, slapping his thigh. "Even on this lousy tape recorder we sound good."

"It's kind of you to blame the tape recorder," Carla said dryly. "But all I seem to hear is me missing my notes. I'm badly out of practice, I'm afraid."

"Rehearsals will take care of that," Drake assured her. "How about I tell my manager to schedule the concert sometime in July? That'll give us over a month to practice."

"Do you think I'll be ready by then?" Carla looked doubtful.

"Sure." He glanced at her and added, "But I need your promise that however discouraged you may get, you won't quit. If you're going to back out, now's the time, not later."

"I won't back out," Carla assured him, surprising herself with her own enthusiasm. "As long as you can promise that my privacy is ensured."

"No problem." He extended his hand. "Deal?"

She took his hand. "Deal. And if we fall flat on our faces you have to promise to pick me up."

"We won't fall flat. We'll stand up and wow 'em," he replied, grinning happily. "Now, our next move is to get you together with the band." For a moment he looked thoughtful. "We need a place where we can practice in secret. Once it's announced that you'll be performing with me, the reporters are going to go wild." He ran his fingers through his brown curls as he pondered. "I know! My parents have a place up at Lake Arrowhead that'll be perfect. Why don't you pack a bag and I'll pick you up Saturday morning, bright and early?"

"I don't know about that . . ." Carla began.

He raised his hand to cut off her protest. "My parents, three brothers and Bobby will be there as chaperones, if that's what's got you so worried."

"Okay, I'll be ready," Carla said. "Pick me up at eight o'clock."

Chapter Five

Carla jerked the laces of her pink running shoes into a bow with a vengeful yank. She was a born worrier, but this time she figured she had reason to worry. When Elizabeth had first suggested the idea of this concert, she had been adamantly opposed. But somehow, someway, Drake had managed to talk her into it, despite her objections and fears.

And it was all her own fault. She shouldn't have let him sing to her. She shouldn't have let him through her front door. She'd known how persuasive he could be.

What had happened? Where had she gone wrong? How had she ended up agreeing to do this concert with him?

Then Elizabeth had dealt another blow: she had informed Carla that she was "temporarily relieved" of her duties as a social worker until after the concert.

"But who'll do my job?" Carla had objected. "We're shorthanded already."

"Not to worry," Elizabeth had responded cheerfully. "Drake's given me some money in advance so I can hire more help. He felt it was crucial for him to have your undivided attention for practice."

With a few quick rips, Drake had torn apart the orderly, carefully controlled routine of Carla's life. Arrangements had already been finalized with the Hollywood Bowl for their concert. Drake's manager was scheduled to break the news of the benefit to the press and television news stations this evening.

Carla was relieved she'd be out of town when that information hit the public. She could imagine the speculation, the questions and the improvised lies about what Carla Fox had been doing, where Carla Fox had been these past ten years.

For a moment she felt a wave of panic. What if no one cared? What if no one wanted to hear her sing? What if she sounded terrible?

The doorbell rang. Carla looked at her watch. Drake was exactly on time.

She looked younger and less businesslike today, Drake noted with approval as Carla opened the door. The pink cotton-knit shirt hugged her breasts, the pink Bermuda shorts and running shoes complemented her trim, shapely legs. She looked soft and feminine—and touchable.

Extending a hand, he stroked the shiny golden strands of her hair. He knew he'd agreed to keep his distance, but the urge to touch her was too compelling.

Carla fought back an irresistible wave of longing—a longing to be touched, a longing to be loved. Reminding herself that she wasn't going to let this man get near her, she ducked her head and backed away. Picking up her suitcase, she suggested brightly, "Shall we go?"

"Here, I'll take that," Drake offered politely, reaching out a hand.

"I know you'll think I'm an ungrateful baggage," Carla joked, "but really, I can handle it myself."

Drake groaned at Carla's pun, adding, "You may be witty, but John Greenleaf was Whittier."

Carla made a face as she walked down the front path. "Shame on you for using such an old joke. I think I first heard that one in the eighth grade."

"I had my mind on more important things than jokes in the eighth grade," Drake replied smoothly.

"Such as girls?" Carla inquired, shooting him a sideways glance.

"You've got it," Drake responded, gesturing toward an old and dented green Chevy station wagon parked at the curb.

"This is your car?" Carla asked, trying to hide the surprise in her voice.

"My other car's a Lotus," Drake replied with a grin.

"Where's Bobby?" Carla asked, peering inside the car. Except for the empty driver and passenger seats, cardboard boxes filled the back of the car.

"He went up yesterday with my mom and dad." The liquid amber of Drake's eyes held Carla still for a moment. Although casually dressed in a T-shirt and running shorts, Drake still managed to exude a compelling and potent masculinity. He raised a dark brow and added with a smile, "As you can see, there wouldn't have been enough room for him with all this stuff."

"How convenient," Carla muttered, ducking her head and climbing into the car.

Even though it was still early morning, the summer sun was already sending out heat that radiated in waves from the black asphalt. The smog-filled air was as murky as smoke and almost as thick and acrid smelling. Carla hoped that the car had air-conditioning. Without it, the four-hour drive to Lake Arrowhead would be intolerable.

Luckily it did. Settling herself back in the surprisingly comfortable seat, Carla watched the scenery as they pulled out.

They passed along street after street and through town after town. They all seemed to blur into one and become faceless, nameless—characterless.

As Drake shifted gears, Carla watched the play of muscles under tanned skin tighten and ripple across his thigh. There was nothing characterless about Drake, she decided. Aggressive and cocky, yes, but not characterless.

"You're quiet this morning," he remarked. "I've been waiting for you to give me hell for the past hour."

"What's the use?" Carla said with a wry smile, nervously fiddling with the black-banded watch on her wrist. "It won't change things. You're going to do what you want no matter how I feel about things."

He started to speak, but his voice seemed to catch for a moment. "Don't you—don't you think I care about your feelings, too?"

Carla turned her head to look at him. His face remained in profile, impossible to read, impossible to interpret. Just this once she wished that she could read his mind as well as he seemed to read hers. Frustration made her say something she didn't really believe herself: "I don't think you care one tiny bit about my feelings."

"You're wrong, you know." This time he turned to look at her, but she had averted her gaze to the houses speeding by outside her window. "I care about you a lot."

Carla's tone was unbelieving. "Why?"

"I don't know," Drake admitted. "Just lucky, I guess."

This time she turned to look at him and was immediately jolted by the current of electricity that sparked in his eyes. Nervously she unfastened the clasp on her watch. "You don't even know me. How could you? We just met a few weeks ago."

"Time isn't always a proper measure for knowing a person," he observed, turning his face toward the road again. "I know you better than you know yourself.

You were born in Paris at the American Hospital. Daniel Fox, your father, died before you were born. At the age of three you made your first movie—"

"You're just giving me statistics," Carla scoffed. "That's not knowing me."

"True," he agreed. "But, since you insist, I'll dig deeper into your past. You gave up music because you believe you're responsible for your mother's death."

"That's nonsense," Carla replied stiffly.

"I'll agree it's a nonsensical idea. But you believe it nevertheless."

"You don't know what you're talking about," Carla replied coldly.

"Don't I? What other reason can you give me for having given up music?"

Looking down at her lap, she noticed the watch she had unconsciously removed. Trying to school indifference into her voice, she replied raggedly, "I got tired of it. I got bored."

"Liar," he softly accused. "Music is in your blood. You didn't walk away from it easily or without a good reason."

She turned her head toward the window once again. Through clenched teeth she said, "It doesn't matter why I left music. It's none of your business."

"Hit too close to home, didn't I?"

Carla tried to mend her splintering composure. Losing her temper would do no good at all. In a voice devoid of inflection, she said, "I wish you'd stop badgering me. If you really cared about me as you say, you wouldn't put me through this."

"If you really cared about yourself, you wouldn't have put yourself through this."

Shifting her body, she crossed her legs. She didn't like talking about herself. It was time to change the subject. "Listen, Drake, we're supposed to be doing a concert together, not shooting each other down. The next six weeks are going to seem very long and trying if we don't agree to cease and desist all military action. I suggest we both make a real effort to try to get along."

"You're right," he agreed. She heard the repetitious clicking sound of his signal light flashing on and off as he wheeled the car into the left-hand turning lane. "I hope you don't mind if we stop for a few minutes. I have to pick up something."

"Don't tell me you forgot something," Carla said in a teasing voice, hoping that a joke might lighten the atmosphere. She twisted her neck to examine the pile of boxes stacked behind her. "I've been expecting one of those boxes to spring a leak any second. I figured the kitchen sink *had* to be in one of them."

Drake just smiled and said nothing as he stopped at a red light. They continued driving toward the town of Pomona.

A few minutes later they arrived at a dilapidated two-story clapboard building with dingy white paint and a dirt driveway. A large pepper tree, trailing long, slender green branches, filled the center of the weed-strewn circular drive. Drake turned in, sending dust flying everywhere and nearly obliterating the sign on the front porch that read Harvey's Secondhand Shop.

A bright blue hand, reminding Carla of a palm reader's sign, was painted next to the lettering.

"What's this?"

Drake's grin was as mysterious as the Mona Lisa's but a lot more gleeful. "Follow me."

Carla waited for the dust to settle before she opened the car door. The heavy scent of dust and spice from the pepper tree was overwhelming.

Drake remained standing by the car, but she could see that it was only consideration for her that was holding him back. The tethered energy he held in control seemed likely to explode at any second.

They clattered up the rickety porch steps and entered through a glass-paned front door. The door hinges screeched and moaned in protest as they walked inside.

The room smelled of must and lemon furniture polish. Carla felt as though she'd entered an old Sears & Roebuck catalogue. A world of the past welcomed her. There were three rooms, and each looked crammed with everything Carla could have imagined and a lot she couldn't have. Books filled glass-fronted bookcases while odd pieces of china were perched on top of an old steamer trunk plastered with enough foreign labels to paper a wall. A dressmaker's form stood next to an old wicker baby buggy, while overhead hung a bird cage and a set of four lyre-back chairs.

"Harvey!" Drake called out. "Where are you?"

"Coming," said a stooped man, shambling into the room. He had weathered features, thin gray hair and a potbelly that hung over a wide, silver-buckled belt.

"Hi, Harvey. I'd like you to meet a friend." Drake gestured to Carla. "Say hello to Carla."

"Pleased to meetcha," Harvey replied, offering her a friendly smile and a firm handshake. He looked her over carefully and seemed to approve. "You're a sight better-lookin' than those no-good brothers of his, and from the looks of you, you've got better manners— you ain't broken nothing yet."

"You know no one would buy any of this junk," Drake said with a sly smile as his hand swept the room, "if they hadn't broken it first."

"True," Harvey agreed cheerfully. "That's why I leave everything in such precarious places. It's the only way I can make any money."

"Speaking of business . . ." Drake began.

"It's in the back room," Harvey said. Noticing the look of wonder on Carla's face as she glanced about, Harvey suggested, "Why don't you come with me and let the lady look around for a while?"

Drake shot Carla an inquiring look, but she was too busy flipping through hangers on a rack of old dresses. There was a lace wedding gown in a size so small it would almost fit a child, a brown wool suit with enough shoulder padding and epaulettes for a four-star general, and several dresses of no particular style or taste.

Then she found it. It was love at first sight. She pulled out a floor-length black velvet strapless evening gown. She'd always loved velvet, loved its shimmering now-you-see-it-now-you-don't quality. She'd always wanted a dress like this. Carla rubbed her cheek against the soft and furry material, then held it up to her, trying to judge if it would fit.

"Go put it on. That dress was made for you," Drake said, seemingly coming from nowhere all of a sudden.

There was mischief in her blue eyes when she looked at him. "Okay, I will. And I'm going to be terribly disappointed if it doesn't fit. I've always wanted a dress like this."

She disappeared into the bathroom Drake pointed out to change into the dress. And it did fit—like a dream.

"I feel like Veronica Lake or maybe even Bette Davis," Carla said with a giggle, when she came floating out of the dressing room.

"Wow," Drake said admiringly. The built-in bra cups on the strapless dress pushed her breasts together, giving her a good amount of rounded cleavage. The skirt was tight and hugged her thighs and had a gaping slit up the side to display her long legs. Drake looked her over appreciatively. "Double and triple wow!" he added, stepping back for a head-to-toe inspection.

"It is beautiful," Carla agreed wistfully, walking over to a wavy antique mirror and looking at herself. She turned and peered over her shoulder to see the view from the back of the dress. "It's a shame I don't have anyplace to wear it."

"Yes, you do." Seeing the questioning look that Carla directed to him, Drake added, "You're forgetting about the concert. It'll be perfect. Why, I even promise to go all out and wear something equally flashy myself."

"That's a deal," Carla said with a laugh, twirling around in a circle joyfully. "I hate to admit it, but I may enjoy doing this concert after all."

Although Drake offered to pay for the dress, Carla firmly refused, handing Harvey a credit card and stating with a laugh, "Candy and flowers are acceptable presents from a gentleman, but a lady never, never accepts clothing."

"Who said I'm a gentleman?" Drake asked, his brown eyes full of merriment.

"Truer words were never spoken," Carla responded quickly. "But that doesn't change anything. I'm still buying my own dress."

Soon they were waving goodbye to Harvey and getting ready to drive on. As they climbed back into the car, Carla noticed that the pile of boxes had been rearranged. Something else had been squeezed into the back of the car.

As Drake started the engine, Carla said, "I didn't get to see what you bought."

"You will." Drake's grin was decidedly boyish. "But later, not now."

It was an unsatisfactory answer. She tried another tack. "You seem to know Harvey well. I gather you're a regular customer."

"That's right. I like old things. They have more character."

Character. That word again. It seemed to come to mind whenever she was near Drake. Eccentric, too. Why would a man with Drake's money and life-style prefer to drive an old Chevy station wagon and frequent a secondhand store?

There were so many questions about Drake. When would she find the answers?

Once again he seemed to read her mind. "I suppose you find it strange that I do my shopping at a secondhand store."

Carla considered this. "I don't think 'strange' is the word I'd use. Maybe 'surprising'."

"I bought my first guitar at a secondhand store," he reminisced, craning his head to check for traffic. Seeing no one, he signaled and changed lanes. "I must have been about ten at the time. The guitar had nylon strings and mother-of-pearl around the sound hole. The finish was scarred and most of the mother-of-pearl had fallen out, but that didn't matter to me. It was still the most beautiful thing I'd ever seen."

A light shone red up ahead. He put on the brakes and stopped, then added, "I wanted lessons so badly, and of course we didn't have the money. There were four of us kids, all boys, and my parents could hardly afford to feed and clothe us. But my mom's a wheeler-dealer."

He looked at Carla briefly before the light turned, and grinned. "I might as well warn you I inherited that trait from her. She's also got a heart of gold. Anyway, Mom was working as a waitress when this musician came into the restaurant. He had a guitar strapped over his back but not a dime for food or a place to stay. When he offered to hock his guitar for a couple of meals, Mom's heart went out to him. She decided to bring him home. We fed him and let him sleep on the couch in exchange for my guitar lessons." Drake shook his head ruefully. "That poor guy sure got ripped off. I was the devil to teach. If my mom hadn't been such a good cook, I'm sure he would never have stuck it out."

"That's a lovely story," Carla said softly.

"Mom's quite a gal. Dad's quite a guy, too, but he's the quiet type. Doesn't talk much. You hardly know he's there. He's always saying that the reason he married Mom was because he knew she'd do all the talking." He turned and, meeting Carla's eyes, added, "Don't you believe it. He worships her. He'd just hate to admit it."

They drove in silence for a few more miles. Soon they passed the city of Redlands and turned north toward the mountains.

The road steepened, becoming narrow and winding. Drake took the hairpin curves as if he knew them well. They were gaining altitude with every minute. Palm trees were replaced by pine trees, suburban housing by rocks and yawning ravines.

"Do you mind if I turn off the air-conditioning?" Drake inquired after a while. "I love the smell of fresh mountain air. It's something you can't buy in stores."

"Go ahead. I wouldn't mind at all," Carla said.

They both rolled down their windows and let the air filter through the car. It was hard to believe that such cool, clean air could exist just a few hours away from the city of Los Angeles. Carla breathed in the fragrant pine smell. Was it the smog or the numbers of people that made Los Angeles sometimes seem so suffocating? And was it the refreshing mountain air or this outgoing yet intensely private man that made her suddenly feel so free and outrageously alive?

By the time they turned onto Rim of the World Drive, they had climbed more than a mile into the mountains. The road continued to turn and twist until it came to Lake Arrowhead and divided in two directions.

They took the north fork that skirted the lake, which reflected blue and silver under a cotton-ball-studded azure sky. Boats dotted the crystal water— some for sailing, some for water skiing, some for just pleasure cruising. Alpine cottages, A-frame houses and rustic log cabins lined the road and shore, along with restaurants, motels, and a Sheraton hotel.

Presently the road wound away from the lake and entered the deep, solemn shade of a pine forest. Carla's eyes would have missed the little road that Drake turned into if the insistent noise from his signal lights hadn't warned her. Next they followed a narrow dirt track with enough rocks and tree branches sticking up from the road to make Carla understand why Drake hadn't taken the Lotus.

They came upon a clearing where a crude hand-painted sign read You're Almost There. Next to the sign was a battered old mailbox with the red flag in the down position. The road continued, eventually ending at a large, rambling house that overlooked the sparkling blue lake.

"We're here," announced Drake. The lilt in his voice told Carla that he was feeling more than his customary joie de vivre.

Carla opened the door and stepped out of the car. Pine trees towered overhead, while the walkway was lined with a profusion of red geraniums. The house, a two-story building with cedar shingles on the sides and roof, was situated far enough from the main road that only the chatter of birds broke the primeval silence.

"It's lovely," Carla said, looking around her, noticing the birdbath and bird feeder set out on the wide green lawn. She breathed deeply, enjoying the smell of fresh-cut grass and cedar trees.

Drake grabbed her hand and impatiently dragged her toward the house. "We'll unpack the car later. I can't wait for you to meet the folks."

If Carla had thought that walking into Harvey's Secondhand Shop was like entering another world, walking into Drake's parents' home was like entering Alice's Wonderland. It was the first of June, and the entire house was decorated for Christmas! There was mistletoe over the chandelier in the vestibule, wreaths and holly were tacked to the knotty pine paneled walls. A giant stuffed Santa stood next to the brass hat-rack.

"Oh, there you are." A gray-haired woman bustled into the room. Her sparkling brown eyes and tanned face reminded Carla of Drake. Barefoot and barelegged, the woman wore red shorts and a kelly-green shirt. Over this was an apron printed with red and green reindeer. She had nice legs and a trim figure, especially for a woman who had obviously reached her sixties. "I thought you'd never get here." She turned from Drake and greeted Carla enthusiastically. "And you're Carla. I'm Mary Lanning, and I'm so happy to meet you. Do you know how to make eggnog?"

"Why, of course," Carla said hesitantly, looking to Drake for assistance. Things were getting curiouser and curiouser each moment.

"Brandy or rum?" Mary demanded.

Carla straightened. Strange situation or not, there could be no question about the answer to *that*. "Why, rum, of course."

"Good. That's what I thought. Come with me." The woman cast Drake a baleful look as if it were all his fault. "Your father wants to put brandy in the eggnog. Imagine! The very idea."

Drake laughed as he hung an arm over his mother's shoulder. "Don't blame me, Mom, blame yourself. You married him. He was your husband before he was my father."

She flashed a grin that was reminiscent of Drake's. "I was young then. So was he. And he was better-looking than you, buddy. Anyway, we all make mistakes."

Carla heard the raucous sound of laughter and male voices as she followed them through the dining room. She also smelled the delicious aroma of roasting turkey and ham. What was going on? The dining room, like the rest of the house, was decorated for Christmas.

"Drake, there you are," came a cry of voices as they entered the kitchen through a swing door. The immense and sunshine-filled room was densely populated with men—the three Lanning brothers, Kevin, Brian and Randy, were on one side: Bobby and an older man whom Carla assumed was Drake's father were at the other.

Introductions were soon made and then Mary waved her hand for silence. "Now, boys." Carla choked back a laugh. Her boys were all at least a foot taller than she. "Carla's come to give her expert opinion. What do you say? Rum or brandy?"

She felt seven pairs of eyes fasten upon her. Seeing the laughter and good humor, Carla smiled and replied, "Why, rum, of course!"

Excitement and pandemonium reigned as Mary, with laughter and a show of great ceremony, poured rum into the crystal bowl placed on a large wooden table in the center of the room. She added a mixture of heavy cream, eggs and sugar, a dash of vanilla and nutmeg and stirred it all together. Then she began ladling the eggnog into matching crystal cups.

"Carla, you as the guest of honor should have the first cup," she announced. Next she looked at Bobby, offered him a cup and then added, "You get the second cup, Bobby, but that's not because you're second best. Family members always come after guests." She winked and then added, "And you'd better make this one last. It's family policy that you aren't allowed a second cup until you reach eighteen.''

"Don't you believe it," Randy broke in. "Drake managed to sneak a second cup once. Mom found out and made him drink a third cup as punishment. He got so sick that he wouldn't drink eggnog again for years."

Everyone laughed and Bobby, who'd been quietly leaning against a pine kitchen cabinet, slowly came forward. He accepted the cup with easy nonchalance, but Carla noticed the wide smile and the happy glow in his eyes when he took the cup and said, "Thanks, Grandma."

There was a burst of applause and then everyone came forward to grab a cup of eggnog. Above the noise, Carla could hear Drake suggesting, "How about a song? Christmas isn't Christmas without music."

Soon they were singing "God Rest Ye Merry Gentlemen." Carla sipped her eggnog and leaned back against a pine paneled cabinet. A warm, gentle breeze fluttered the red and white gingham curtains framing the kitchen window. She could see all the familiar signs of summer—sunshine dappling green pine trees, honeybees buzzing in colorful flowers, a squirrel running up a tree. Why were they pretending it was Christmas?

They seemed to know all the words to all the Christmas songs. Carla watched as the eggnog in the punch bowl became lower and lower. If it was possible, their laughter and singing seemed to grow stronger and stronger.

Their joy and good spirits were infectious. Mystified by everything though she was, Carla couldn't help joining in the celebration. They were a close-knit but welcoming family. It was impossible not to feel part of them.

An end finally came, as it does to all good things. The punch bowl and glasses were empty. Mary Lanning waved her hands for silence. "The fun's over for a while. Why don't you boys unpack Drake's car while I show Carla to her room? We'll also need firewood and a fire for the living room."

"It's too warm for a fire," Brian objected. He was tall, like all the Lanning men, but he was the only blonde of the bunch.

"It's Christmas. You can't have Christmas without a fire," she rebutted. "Turn the air-conditioning on extra high."

Carla followed Mary through the house, past an enormous pine-paneled living room with braided rag rugs and comfortable-looking chintz-covered furniture, up a carpeted staircase with an intricately carved banister, and down a long hall to a room at the end. Family pictures cluttered the hall walls and piqued Carla's interest.

As they walked, Drake's mother kept up a steady stream of talk. It ranged from everything to the president's last political speech to how Bobby had forgotten to pack his underwear.

"He told me that he'd lived in one pair of underwear for weeks and not to worry about it," Mary explained. "But of course that wouldn't do. So we ran into Blue Jay and bought out the general store. And that's why I'm behind schedule. I should have had all my mince pies done by now."

"This is your room," Mary said as they stopped in front of a door. Suddenly realizing that she had flour on her hands, she wiped her hands across her apron. "I hope you like it. The boys sleep out in the cabins, but they're a bit rough and rustic. I thought you might appreciate something a bit more feminine and elegant."

"It's beautiful," Carla said as she walked into the room. A large brass bed dominated the shining wide-planked pine floor. Upon the bed lay a wedding-ring quilt in white and pastel colors. Dainty blue and white wallpaper covered the walls, while white lace-edged Priscilla curtains billowed in the windows.

"I decorated it myself," Drake's mother confessed. "I love pretty things, but they're not always practical when you have four boys." She shot Carla an embarrassed look. "I'm not complaining, mind you. My boys have always been great. But lace isn't quite their thing."

Carla plunked herself down on the bed and let her fingers enjoy the cushiony softness of the quilt. Her voice sounded dreamy, a far cry from her usual businesslike tones. "I love quilts. There's so much love in them. Such feeling and character." Carla stopped herself momentarily, realizing the word fit Drake's mother as well as Drake himself.

"I'm glad you like it. I thought I would never get it finished."

"You made it?" Carla gasped in surprise.

Mary nodded, looking surprisingly shy for a moment.

Carla thought about the past hour since she'd arrived—the fun, the warmhearted laughter. As a child she had desperately longed for a family like this, and now she finally had a chance to be part of them for a short while.

There was only one thing left that was still bothering her.

Carla twisted the watchband on her arm. Raising her eyes, she looked Mary straight in the face and said, "There's one thing that's got me curious. It's the first of June. Why are we celebrating Christmas?"

Chapter Six

Mary's response to Carla's question was a total surprise. A look of shock and disbelief covered Mary's face momentarily, then she gave a quick gurgle of laughter. Her laughter grew and grew until finally she pulled up a cane-back rocking chair and sat down, doubled over with laughter.

"Please excuse me," Mary gasped, laughing so hard that there were tears in her eyes. She took a deep breath and said, "I know I'm being rude, but it's oh so-o-o funny."

That set up another bout of laughter. Puzzled, Carla remained seated on the bed and waited for Mary to continue.

At last Mary had control of herself. Straightening herself up, she said, "I always knew Drake was a mischief maker, but this is too much. Oh! He's bad! I can't believe even he would do such a mean thing. What must you think of us?" Running a finger along the green piping that edged the pocket on her apron, she looked at Carla and added, "I gather Drake didn't tell you that we were doing this for Bobby?"

"No," Carla replied, shaking her head, still looking mystified.

"The rascal." Mary smiled. "We've been waiting to do this for months—sort of as a celebration for Bobby becoming a real member of the family. You see, Bobby once told Drake that he'd never had a happy Christmas in his life. Drake decided that since there were so many Christmases to make up for, we'd have two this year."

"What a nice idea," said Carla, the light of understanding dawning on her face.

"Naturally I assumed he'd told you," Mary explained with a grin.

"Naturally," Carla agreed with a smile and a nod. "You'd expect that. Any normal person would have told me. But not Drake."

The sound of voices and the clomping of feet pounding along the wood-floored hallway interrupted them. As the women shifted their eyes to the doorway, Drake marched into the room carrying Carla's suitcase.

"Hi," he greeted cheerfully as he bent over to drop the suitcase gently on the floor. He straightened. "You ladies having fun getting acquainted?"

"Drake, that was a dirty trick you pulled on Carla," Mary scolded, standing up and smoothing out the folds of her apron with her hands. She tried to hide a smile as she shook an admonishing finger at him. "You ought to be ashamed of yourself."

Drake's laughter filled the room. "I know, Mom, but I couldn't resist. You should have seen the look on Carla's face when we started to sing 'It's Beginning to Look a Lot Like Christmas'! It was absolutely priceless."

"Priceless, perhaps, but in very bad taste. I thought I raised you better than that," Mary said with a sniff, thrusting her hands on her hips and shaking her head ruefully. "I expect you to apologize."

"Please forgive me," Drake pleaded. His dark-brown eyes bubbled with merriment as he placed a hand over his heart and added melodramatically, "I promise I'll never do it again."

Carla couldn't help laughing. "That's an empty promise if ever I heard one. I'm not about to fall for that trick again."

"Now that we've got all that straightened out," Mary began as she started for the door, "how about you kids doing me a favor? We need a Christmas tree. Would you like to go find one?"

"That sounds like a good plan to me." Drake looked at Carla. "How about you? Want to come along?"

"No more practical jokes?" Carla asked with a mock-stern look.

"Promise." Raising a hand, Drake pledged solemnly, "Scout's honor."

"I wouldn't take that promise too seriously," Mary interjected from the doorway. "Drake was kicked out of scouts at the age of ten for slipping a garter snake in the den mother's purse."

"Mom, don't you have some cooking to do?" Drake inquired with a raised brow. "You're not supposed to tell all my guilty secrets."

"I couldn't possibly. It would take years to tell them all," was Mary's final parting shot. Then she was gone.

"Care to take a chance anyway?" Drake asked with a teasing, amused look in his eyes.

"Why not?" Carla responded quickly.

Drake raked his eyes over Carla's attire, noting her slender hips and the straight lines of slim legs beneath her shorts. "As much as I enjoy the lovely view of your legs, you'll have to change first. You need something that covers them."

"That shouldn't take long," Carla promised. "I'll change and meet you at the top of the staircase in five minutes."

It took her only a few minutes to slip out of her shorts and climb into a pair of beige Levi's. She tied back her long hair with a narrow white silk scarf, ensuring that the jagged scar line on her scalp where the hair wouldn't grow was hidden from view.

"Why did you do it?" Carla asked Drake a few minutes later. Her rubber-soled running shoes made a soft, padding sound as they hit the carpeted stairs.

"Do what?" Drake gave her a questioning glance. He also had changed from his running shorts to a pair of worn and faded blue jeans.

Carla shot him an amused look as she shook her head ruefully. "Don't play innocent with me. It's unconvincing and out of character. I want to know why you didn't explain to me beforehand the reason you were having this Christmas party. I'll admit you had me going for a few minutes. I couldn't quite decide if I was the one who was crazy or if all of you were crazy instead."

"Oh, that." Drake glanced at her and grinned. "I thought it would make a nice surprise. I thought it might make you laugh. You're much too serious, you know."

"There seems to be a lot wrong with me," Carla muttered. She waited as he opened the front door for her. His display of chivalry surprised her.

"There's nothing wrong with you that the Lanning family can't cure," he said, the mocking glint of laughter in his eyes nullifying his recent show of good manners. "I figure a month with us and you'll be either crazy or cured. And probably both."

"What a lot I have to look forward to. I can hardly wait," Carla remarked dryly as she followed Drake along a path that bordered the back of the house. The shining mirror surface of the lake was to their right. To the left stretched a swimming pool filled with glistening aqua-blue water, and an asphalt tennis court.

"I'm glad you see it that way."

"Do I have a choice?" Carla asked good-naturedly, kicking a stone along the path.

"Not really," he said with a chuckle. "Or at least, not for the next six weeks."

They walked on, following a rock-studded path as it twisted and turned. A pine-log cabin loomed ahead and to the right. It was situated so close to the lake that it seemed ready to topple into the water at any moment. Just in front of the cabin was a dock with a canoe and a sailboat moored to the pilings.

Carla breathed in the cedar-scented air. "I love this place. Tell me more about it. Is it all yours?"

"It's all my parents'," Drake corrected. He didn't bother to tell her that he'd actually bought the property and given it to his parents. "It used to be a sort of lodge motel. We stayed here one summer when we were kids. It was ramshackle, run-down, and we loved it."

Carla thought about the impeccable and expensive hotels she'd visited with her mother as a child. There'd never been anything to do in them but watch TV and call room service. "You're lucky to have such a wonderful, homey place."

"It's worked out well for the family," Drake agreed. "Mom and Dad live in the main house, my brothers and I stay in the cabins. Nobody gets on anybody's nerves. Everybody has a place of their own. It leaves us free to come and go as we want."

"Which cabin is yours?" Carla asked, craning her neck to get a better view of the six cabins nestled in a row along the lake.

"That one." Drake pointed ahead to the last cabin in the row. "We call it Comanche. All of the cabins are named after Indian tribes. And over there, through the trees, is Cherokee. That's our sound studio, where we'll be practicing for the concert."

Carla halted, shading her eyes from the sunlight glancing through the trees. "I was wondering when we'd get around to practicing. I gather that's not on the agenda for today?"

"We start Monday morning," Drake informed her. "And you'd better be ready because I plan to work you hard."

"I figured as much. You don't strike me as a man who does things halfway."

"Halfway is no way," Drake responded cheerfully. "Come on, let's go find us a Christmas tree."

The weather was perfect. Warm but not hot. The clear blue sky made everything seem clean and crisp and shining. The air around them was redolent of the scent of wild flowers, cedar and pine. As Drake stopped to point out a yellow mustard flower, Carla said, "Drake, I owe you an apology." Batting away a branch that had grown over the path, she continued, "I was totally out of line in rejecting your request to adopt Bobby. It's obvious you're going to make an excellent parent. Bobby seems so happy with your family. I can see an improvement in him already."

"Don't judge yourself too harshly on that," Drake remarked, turning to look at her. "I guess I didn't exactly come across as the ideal father type, what with Angie being there and my calling you a terminal virgin."

"I'd forgotten about you calling me *that*," Carla said with a laugh. "I take it all back. I don't owe you any apologies at all."

He laughed too and directed his eyes back to the trees. Sunlight filtered through the forest, leaving patterns of light and dark against his face. Shading his eyes with a hand, he added, "Have you ever gone looking for a Christmas tree before?"

"Sure. Every year I go looking for one at the YMCA lot near my house," Carla replied.

"That's not the same thing at all," Drake said, running fingers through his shaggy brown hair. "That's like store-bought bread versus homemade. They both have the same name, but the smell and the texture are worlds apart."

"And I suppose homegrown Christmas trees taste different, too," Carla teased.

"That's right," Drake said, a serious look crossing his face. "The smell of a fresh tree is so wonderfully overpowering that you can practically taste it. Just like the smell of homemade bread."

"If you say so." Carla looked around her and pointed to a tree a few feet back from the path. "Would that tree be okay?"

"You've got to be kidding!" Drake said, shaking his head.

Carla looked annoyed. It seemed like a lovely tree to her. "Why not? It's an evergreen. It has a nice shape. What's wrong with it?"

"It's tall enough to put in a department store, that's what's wrong with it. Come here and I'll show you," he said, stepping off the path and walking toward the tree.

"I guess it is a wee bit tall," Carla admitted, craning her neck to look up at the tree, which towered over the two of them. It was easily twenty feet high.

Drake had wandered off to a clump of bushes nearby. He returned shortly, hands behind his back. "Carla, close your eyes."

"Why?" she demanded, looking at him with curiosity.

His brown eyes twinkled. "Close your eyes and you'll find out."

"If this is another one of your tricks . . ."

"It's not. I promise. Now, do what I say. Close your eyes."

She shut her eyes reluctantly.

"Now open your mouth," Drake said.

Her eyes flew open. "I won't! I don't trust you."

"Trust me," he coaxed. "Now, do what I say. Close your eyes and open your mouth."

She did. Then she felt the touch of his fingers against her lips and teeth, and the taste of something tart and sweet.

"Mmm, blackberries. I haven't had any in years," she said, chewing.

"Ready for another?" he asked, pressing a berry against her lips. She opened her mouth. This blackberry was so ripe that it burst as she closed her teeth on it. The sweet taste exploded in her mouth as clear purple juices dribbled down her chin. She opened her eyes.

"Hold still," Drake ordered. With a gentle stroke of his finger, he wiped the juice away and put his finger to her mouth so she could lick the remaining sweetness.

"Would you like another?" he asked softly.

"Yes, please." Her voice was husky. She was very aware of his closeness; very aware of him as a man.

"Close your eyes again."

She closed her eyes and waited for the solid warmth of his fingers against her mouth. They never came. Instead, she felt the softness of his lips molding to hers, and the curve of his tongue as he gently pressed a succulent blackberry into her mouth.

She was aware of a multitude of contradictory things—tartness and sweetness, softness and firmness, strength and tenderness. She felt his hands smoothly caress her body as the warm afternoon sun splayed around them.

A motorboat roared by on the lake. The harsh noise distracted her long enough to remember who she was, who he was, and that he had made a promise not to touch her. She broke away.

"I think we'd better move on," she said raggedly, digging her hands into her back pants pockets. "We've got a Christmas tree to find."

Without another word he led the way down the path again. It was a beautiful, peaceful kind of day. A gentle breeze rustled the branches in the trees. Squirrels chattered and ran along the path. Overhead a blue jay squawked and cawed.

Carla spotted a tree a few yards back from the path. "How about that one?" she suggested.

"Not bad," Drake said, stopping and regarding it critically.

"Not bad? It's perfect," Carla defended irately, tromping through the undergrowth. She circled the tree slowly, noticing its shape and the sturdiness of its branches and green needles. "Oh, look, it's got pinecones on it. Isn't that adorable?"

"Absolutely adorable," Drake said, looking at her instead. He watched her as she surveyed the tree. There was a happy, childlike excitement about her that he'd never seen before. Her blue eyes were shining as brightly as Christmas-tree ornaments under a blaze of lights. Bright smudges of pink color painted her cheeks. Her elegantly tapered fingers were constantly on the go, touching a branch here, touching a branch there. He couldn't help but wonder what it would be like to have those agile and eloquent hands of hers on his body.

She was beautiful, Drake thought. But beauty meant little to him. After all, he lived in a town where outward beauty was more common than rare.

But Carla had an inner beauty, he decided; a sensitivity and depth that he found both fascinating and mysterious. And despite the secrets and sadness he often saw reflected in her eyes, she had the strength of character to be able to look at the world as it was and still laugh.

Drake shook himself out of his reverie as he realized Carla was watching him with questioning eyes. He said, "There's one more critical test before we make the final decision."

"Test?" Carla put her hands on her hips and looked at him questioningly.

His mouth twisted in a smile. "I've always felt that the view from underneath a Christmas tree was very important. I guess that goes back to the time when I was ten. Mom had warned us all year that there was no money for presents. So when I woke up that morning, I promised myself I wasn't going to cry when I saw no presents under the Christmas tree. After all, I was the eldest, I was expected to set a good example." He hesitated, his eyes taking on a faraway expression.

"Yes," Carla prodded. She liked hearing stories of his childhood. Unlike the stories of her childhood, they always seemed to have happy endings. "What happened?"

"I walked into the living room. Underneath the tree was the biggest, fanciest electric train set you can imagine." Noticing Carla's quizzical look, he explained, "Mom had told the truth. There was no money for presents. She'd neglected to mention that she'd won a train set in a contest. After all, she was always entering contests. We used to kid her about the amount of money she wasted on postage. No one expected her to win.

Taking Carla's hand in his, he motioned for her to lie down on the pine-needle-strewn forest floor. "You can imagine our reactions when we saw that train set. Dad had stayed up all night to set the thing up. There were all kinds of trestles and bridges and buildings winding around the stem of that tree. It was set out as neat and perfect as Disneyland, only smaller." He smiled for a moment and then went on, "I remember lying down on those train tracks and looking up at the Christmas tree to give thanks. I can still recall the sparkle of flashing colored lights and the tangy smell of pine from that tree. I can still remember the feel of sticky sap oozing down my face. Most of all," he said with a grin, "I remember one of my brothers turning on the train set. He almost electrocuted me to death."

"But like the cat with nine lives you survived," Carla added. She looked up to see the blue sky and the sun peeking through the branches. Had she ever felt so happy? Had she ever felt so peaceful yet alive? She didn't think so.

"Yes, I survived," said Drake, interrupting her thoughts. "Just like you. We have a lot in common, you know."

"Oh, Drake, I wish that were really true," Carla said with a sigh, as she looked up and saw a blue sky through the canopy of branches. She reached out a hand and pulled a branch to her nose. After breathing in the tangy pine smell she let go of the branch, watching as it sprang back into place. "You're such a happy, giving kind of person. I'd love to be able to look at life through your eyes."

"You can," Drake said, rolling over and sidling his body close to her. His hand caught her chin and directed her eyes to his face. "All you have to do is look in my eyes and try."

Carla gazed at him, noticing the curve of a smile on his lips and the tanned skin stretched tightly across his cheekbones. But it was the look in his eyes that made her pulse flutter and caused her to take in a sharp, ragged breath. She felt as though the warm glow in his eyes penetrated her soul, and her spirits seemed to lift and soar. She murmured, "You're right. I can feel it. I can see it. What a beautiful place this world of ours is!"

Drake felt heady with success, as if he'd just discovered the secret of eternal happiness. To see her vivid blue eyes no longer clouded with secrets and sadness was a gift beyond compare.

Carla felt her pulse begin to hammer. He was so near, so close. And he was right. They did have something in common: a bond, an intangible something that drew them together. Despite their different backgrounds, there was a closeness between them that could not be explained.

Drake leaned over and gently brushed a strand of blond hair away from her face. It was his tenderness that won her. If he had grabbed her, if he had been just a little bit impatient, she would have rejected him. But she had known so little tenderness in her life. She had often yearned for tenderness, and had even wanted to give it, but like many things that are desperately wanted, it had always remained just out of her grasp and experience. So how could she deny it now, especially when his eyes were looking at her with such love and compassion?

"Hello, Carla," he whispered.

"Hello," she answered back. "You're too far away. Come closer."

He leaned over and pressed his lips against hers. She hadn't known that a kiss could be so soft, so subtle, so seductive. His lips barely whispered across her mouth, then they murmured up to her eyes and brow. The journey finally ended at her ears. With a feathering, delicate stroke, he caressed one ear and then the other.

His lips were more insistent when they made their return—but still teasing, still in control. His tongue darted in and out of her mouth, then playfully rimmed the edge of her lips. She felt the scrape of his teeth against her mouth and then a gentle bite as they nibbled on her lower lip.

He was slow—achingly slow. Her breathing was short and ragged as she ran her fingers along the soft cotton of his shirt and felt the firm, male line of solid muscle and sharp bones from his rib cage.

Her fingers barely hesitated when they reached the waistband of his pants. Deciding in an instant, she pulled his T-shirt free of his jeans. Now she could feel the pulsing warmth of his flesh under her fingertips. Now she could be as close to him as possible. It was what she wanted. It was what she needed. It was what she had to have.

An arm reached out to push her hand away. "Take it easy, Carla," he rasped. His luminescent brown eyes were as steady on hers as a lover's kiss. "There's no need to rush things. I want you to be sure you know what you're doing."

"Shhh," she said, putting a finger to his lips. Hungrily his lips nibbled at her fingers. "Please don't make trouble," she begged. "Things are already complicated enough as it is."

He felt the way her need for him made her tremble beneath his hand. It humbled him and made him want to handle her very carefully. She reminded him of rare and carefully crafted crystal. Strong yet fragile. Beautiful yet brittle.

She had seen so much trouble, so much pain. But it hadn't broken her spirit. Her cautious reserve was only skin-deep; beneath it beat the soul of a passionate and sensitive woman.

He wanted to be the one to free her. He wanted to be the one to make it up to her. But first he had to learn the secrets of her heart. He longed to know what still tortured her.

Her blue eyes were stormy and impatient. Nevertheless, he took his time. Rushing would never win her. Reaching out, he slowly stroked the line of her shoulder to her neckline. She was soft beneath his touch, silky.

Carla was only dimly aware of the stones and sticks that dug into her back as she lay upon the forest floor. All she was aware of was a fire that raged at the core of her and threatened to melt her very flesh.

"You're impatient, aren't you," he said teasingly, reading the longing in her eyes. Easing his body sideways, he covered her. He liked the feel of her hips cradling his. She felt small and light and fit tightly beneath him.

His hands followed the curved line of her hips and the narrow funnel of her waist. He continued slowly upward, stopping at her breasts. Here he lingered, rubbing his fingers along the delicate, lacy fabric of her bra until she was quivering with need.

"You're so beautiful. Oh, so beautiful," Drake whispered while slowly unbuttoning her shirt. His hands stopped momentarily at the last button as he took a deep breath. Then, gently, he slipped his fingers under the fabric and pulled the shirt away.

His eyes feasted on the sight of her two dusky pink nipples peeping through the transparent lace of her bra. He leaned over and tasted a nipple, unmindful of the cloth against his tongue. As his lips continued their pillage, moving determinedly upward, his hands continued to search the rounded nape of her neck and the fine, fragile bones of her face.

"Have you ever made love beneath a Christmas tree?" Drake asked, bending lower to kiss her. His voice was as deep and thick as velvet.

"N-no," Carla stammered after a long pause. His lips touched hers once again.

"Neither have I. Would you like to give it a try?"

"I thought you'd never ask," Carla replied. Slipping her hands around his back, she slid her fingers beneath the waistband of his jeans. She pressed him to her, liking the feel of his lean, muscular buttocks filling her hands.

Although the day was not exceedingly warm, a thin layer of perspiration made their bodies cling to one another like sweet honey on hungry fingers. Carla felt Drake's heavy, labored breathing fan and heat her face. His clean scent surrounded her.

Still, Drake took his time. Easing his way down Carla's body, he stopped at her waist. Slowly, much too slowly, he unfastened her jeans.

"Faster," Carla urged, lifting her body and impatiently tugging her jeans over her hips.

"What's your hurry?" Drake asked with a slight, tender smile. His large hands, callused from hours of guitar playing, overlapped hers and slowed the unsheathing of her jeans.

"You're teasing me," she playfully accused him as his hands stopped hers at the tops of her thighs.

"No, I'm just being cautious." He laughed, leaning over and planting a lingering kiss on her mouth once again. "I just want to make sure you really want me. Tell me, Carla, do you really want me?"

"Quit playing hard to get." She smiled into his eyes. "It's out of character and unconvincing." Wedging her knee between his legs, she began to massage gently. "That role doesn't suit you."

"What role does suit me?" Drake inquired as he tugged her jeans off.

Her answer was muffled by his kiss.

"Oh, Carla," he rasped, as his lips pulled away from hers. "You're driving me crazy. I never knew it could be like this."

"Neither did I," Carla murmured. She'd never felt so loved, so safe. She'd never felt that things could ever be so right.

Drake's hands slid up and pulled the scarf out of Carla's hair while he gently ground his hips over hers. Moaning, she arched toward him as he added, "I want your hair down and flowing over your shoulders when we make love."

"Whatever you want," she said.

He settled his knees beside her hips, then leaned over and threaded his hands into the gleaming yellow strands of her hair. He leaned even closer, nuzzling his lips against her scalp as he gently stroked her hair.

Suddenly he sucked in his breath and in an incredulous tone, said, "My poor, lovely, Carla. Whatever happened to your head? You've got scars running across your scalp that look like a road map!"

Carla struggled to get up from her reclining position. She took a deep breath, trying to suppress the wave of nausea deluging her senses. Think about something else—anything else, she commanded herself sternly. Looking around, she snatched up her scarf from where it lay discarded, and with trembling hands, replaced it on her head. The years of lies and deceptions and pretending that life was wonderful came to the foreground. She said shakily, "Oh, that, it's nothing. I was injured as a kid. I fell off my bicycle."

Drake looked at her skeptically, noting her pale face and the way her hands were shaking. Her blue eyes were shuttered and lifeless. She was lying, but why?

Carla stood and hurriedly began to put on her clothes. As she shoved an arm into one of her shirt sleeves, Drake asked, "What's wrong? What's happened? Why are you so upset?"

"Please. I was wrong. I'm not ready for this. All I want you to do is leave me alone," Carla replied in a high-pitched, slightly hysterical tone of voice. She hesitated a moment, trying to recover her equilibrium, then added, "You broke your promise not to touch me. I'm giving you fair warning: next time you break it, I'm leaving."

"Now, wait a minute," Drake broke in angrily, "I asked you if it was all right. You positively begged me—"

"I said, let's not talk about it," Carla implored between clenched teeth. "You get one more chance. But if you slip again, I'm gone!"

As Carla hurried down the path that led to the main house, she knew herself to be a liar and a hypocrite. She had wanted him—oh, how she'd wanted him! But he'd gotten too close. How could she have been so careless as to let him look at her hair!

She'd have to be much, much more careful with him in the future. If it was possible.

Chapter Seven

Christmas in June at the Lanning home was an experience Carla would never forget. The whole family joined in the fun of pretending it was Christmas, which consisted of a lot of lighthearted banter and teasing.

Everyone had gathered in the living room to decorate the tree. The room was a cheerful and rustic room, with a wood-beamed cathedral ceiling, wagon-wheel chandelier, pine-paneled walls and rag rugs. One long wall was lined with built-in bookcases filled with books. A blazing fire burned in the stone fireplace, warming a room made chilly by air-conditioning.

Carla, comfortably ensconced on a blue and white chintz couch, was stringing cranberries for the tree, and had a ringside view of the festivities.

"Drake, must you play that schmaltzy Bing Crosby Christmas record?" Brian grumbled as he tested a string of Christmas-tree lights on the living room floor. Brian was tall and muscular like Drake, but instead of his hair being dark-brown, it was almost as blond as Carla's. Brian was more classically handsome than Drake, but Carla didn't find him nearly as attractive. He lacked Drake's compelling, magnetic brand of energy. Brian shoved a plug into the wall socket, then watched the tree lights flicker on and then twinkle. Noticing several lights that were inoperative, he leaned over and rummaged for spare bulbs in a large box full of Christmas supplies. He flashed a typical Lanning grin and asked, "What would your fans think if they knew you had such lousy taste in music?"

Drake, who with Bobby's help was trying to get the tree to stay upright in its stand, smiled at his brother and said, "Every year you gripe about that record. Every year you threaten to throw it out. And every year you somehow manage to forget. Methinks you protest too much. I bet you really like it."

"Don't take these guys too seriously," Randy advised. He was busy sorting through boxes of ornaments. Like the rest of the brothers, he was casually dressed in a T-shirt and blue jeans. "Arguing about that record has become a family tradition. They've been doing it since they were kids."

"We've worn out three Bing Crosby records in the process," Drake cut in. He stepped back to look at the tree. It stood straight and tall and its clean pine smell filled the room.

"Not bad," Kevin said admiringly, looking up from his job of stringing popcorn. "It sure beats the tree Drake picked last December. It was so bald at the back that we had to hide it in a corner." He picked up two pieces of popcorn, popped one into his mouth and stabbed the other with a needle. "What do you say, guys, shall we make Carla our official Christmas-tree finder?"

"I'll second that motion." Drake grinned. "All in favor?"

The chorus of approval was deafening.

Carla looked up from her cranberry stringing and smiled, but said nothing. She knew they were just teasing. It was all just a pipe dream. Next Christmas she'd be back in her old rut, alone except for Elizabeth and the kids.

Still, she couldn't help wishing that it would really happen. She'd like to be more than just a visitor to this family. They were so happy together; they enjoyed themselves and each other. She could just imagine what a different person she'd be if she'd grown up in a family like theirs.

Drake saw the play of emotions crossing her face. He could read her thoughts as if they were in two-inch boldface print. Give us time, he silently pleaded to her. Give us a chance. We have so much love to give. There's plenty enough for you.

Especially in my heart, he added to himself. Sauntering across the room, he stopped in front of Carla and extended a hand. "Come on, beautiful lady. It's time we got down to business. As guest of honor, it's your job to put the angel on the top of the tree."

"Me?" Carla said, looking embarrassed but pleased.

Drake pulled her up and into his arms. Carla felt her pulse begin to hammer as she bumped against the solid strength of him. She knew that her face must be as red as the bow on the Christmas wreath hanging over the fireplace. Suddenly embarrassed at what his family might be thinking, she took a step back.

She walked over to the Christmas tree, Drake following at her heels. Craning her neck toward the ceiling, she noticed how tall the tree was. It would never have fit into the room if they hadn't cut the top off.

"I'll never reach the top without a chair," Carla said decisively. Her gaze swept the room, looking for a sturdy nonupholstered chair.

"You don't need a chair," Drake replied with a mischievous glint to his eyes. "I'll help you instead."

She should have been wary, she should have known that he'd have an ulterior motive. Still, she was completely unprepared when he stooped down and grabbed her by the knees.

When he straightened up, she stood at least eight feet tall. To her utter chagrin, the whole family was watching with wholehearted, fascinated glee.

"Why, she's high on Drake," someone said with a snicker.

"What a lowering thought," Carla quipped. She leaned over, trying to maintain her balance against Drake's torso and shoulders.

"Here's the angel." Drake's youngest brother, Kevin, handed Carla a porcelain-faced doll with a long bell skirt of white satin and lace. Stiff wire kept the white satin-and-lace wings on the angel's back upright.

"Thanks," Carla replied with a grimace. She was finding it hard to breathe. Whether it was because of Drake's tight grip on her body or his close proximity, she couldn't tell.

Drake tottered toward the tree while Carla tried not to lose her balance. As the room swam drunkenly before her eyes, Carla couldn't help laughing at the absurdity of the situation. Drake stopped in front of the tree, and Carla, almost weak from laughter, leaned over and put the angel on the top.

Slowly, ever so slowly, Drake lowered her, letting her body slide against his. Her heart beat erratically as their bodies brushed against one another and she heard the quick intake of Drake's breath as her feet touched the floor. Then he leaned over and kissed her.

She should have been accustomed to his kisses already, but she wasn't. His energy, his incredible vitality, pulsed into her and demanded all she had—and more. There was no way to deny him.

The fire spat and sighed as a log tumbled in the fireplace. Realizing that Drake's family must be watching, she stepped back and managed to say,

. . . be tempted!

See inside for special
4 FREE BOOKS offer

Silhouette Special Edition™

Discover deliciously different romance with 4 Free Novels from

Silhouette Special Edition™

Sit back and enjoy four exciting romances—yours **FREE** from Silhouette Books! But wait . . . there's *even more* to this great offer! You'll also get . . .

A COMPACT MANICURE SET—ABSOLUTELY FREE! You'll love your beautiful manicure set—an elegant and useful accessory to carry in your handbag. Its rich burgundy case is a perfect expression of your style and good taste—and it's yours free with this offer!

PLUS A FREE MYSTERY GIFT—A surprise bonus that will delight you!

You can get all this just for trying Silhouette Special Edition!

MONEY-SAVING HOME DELIVERY!

Once you receive your 4 FREE books and gifts, you'll be able to preview more great romance reading in the convenience of your own home at less than retail prices. Every month we'll deliver 6 brand-new Silhouette Special Edition novels right to your door months before they appear in stores. If you decide to keep them, they'll be yours for only $2.25 each! That's 50¢ less per book than what you pay in stores—with no additional charges for home delivery!

SPECIAL EXTRAS—FREE!

You'll also get our monthly newsletter, packed with news of your favorite authors and upcoming books—FREE! And as a valued reader, we'll be sending you additional free gifts from time to time—as a token of our appreciation.

BE TEMPTED! COMPLETE, DETACH AND MAIL YOUR POSTPAID ORDER CARD TODAY AND RECEIVE 4 FREE BOOKS, A MANICURE SET AND A MYSTERY GIFT—PLUS LOTS MORE!

A FREE
Manicure Set
and Mystery Gift *await you, too!*

✓ Clip and mail this postpaid card today!

⬭ Silhouette Special Edition™

Silhouette Books
901 Fuhrmann Blvd., P.O. Box 9013, Buffalo, NY 14240-9963

☐ **YES!** Please rush me my four Silhouette Special Edition novels with my FREE Manicure Set and Mystery Gift, as explained on the opposite page. I understand that I am under no obligation to purchase any books. The free books and gifts remain mine to keep.

235 CIC R1WS

NAME _____
(please print)

ADDRESS _____ APT. _____

CITY _____ STATE _____ ZIP _____

PRINTED IN U.S.A.

"That's some mistletoe. I think you should have it X-rated."

That made everyone laugh. Drake looked around him and said, "I'm getting hungry. And I know Mom won't feed us until we get this tree decorated. Anybody want to help?"

This was greeted with a chorus of approval. Suddenly everyone was everywhere.

It was Mary's job to distribute ornaments to the decorators. As she handed them out, she told Carla and Bobby the history of each one—the misshapen tinfoil star Kevin had made in the third grade; the stuffed Santa Claus Drake had made in the seventh grade. Mary went on and on, telling story after story. Carla was fascinated and slightly envious.

The Christmases of her childhood had always been unpredictable. One year, if Carla was in her mother's good graces, she'd be deluged with parents and loving talk. The next year, or the year after that, her mother would be angry with her. So Carla would receive no presents and there would be no Christmas tree. "Switches for witches," her mother would say with a wicked look in her vivid blue eyes, the bright red line of her lipstick a cruel slash of color against her heavily made-up face. "You've been bad this year. You don't deserve anything but punishment."

It was the uncertainty of Christmas that had always been so difficult for Carla. The waiting, the not knowing what would happen. She had always longed for a loving, happy family—one like Drake's family. But instead she'd gotten her mother, with her quicksilver moods that could go from good to bad in the blink of an eye.

But that was all in the past, she reminded herself. And now she had the opportunity—and the honor— of celebrating Christmas in June with a kind, loving family.

At last the tree, with all its ornaments, brilliant colored lights and silver tinsel, was finished. Drake picked up his Gibson guitar and sat down on the floor next to the tree. Motioning for everyone to join him, Drake began to sing "Oh Christmas Tree."

Bobby was the first to join in, and Carla and the rest of the family added their voices to the chorus. As they began to sing yet another round of Christmas carols, Carla exchanged a happy grin with Bobby. His face was as animated as any child's at Christmas. Carla was glad she was there to see him happy and filled with a joy he would never have had at the orphanage.

Drake's father came into the room carrying the crystal punch bowl, filled once again with eggnog. Mary followed in his wake, talking as she walked. "Now, be careful, Henry, don't trip when you get to the rug. Remember, you did that last winter and you had a sprained ankle for a month."

"It wasn't sprained," Drake's father grumbled. "Just slightly twisted. You kept saying it was sprained so you'd have an excuse to baby me."

"Slightly twisted, my eye!" Mary said vehemently. "I know you, Henry Lanning. If you were dying of pneumonia you'd claim it was hay fever. Now, set that bowl down on the table gently before you break it. I'll ladle us up some eggnog."

This was the best Christmas of her life, Carla thought moments later, leaning back against her chair and sipping her eggnog. The fact that it was being celebrated in June just made it all the nicer.

She looked across the room, hoping to catch Drake's eye. Carla nodded and flashed him a happy smile. He responded with a broad one of his own. A warm feeling enveloped her, and she knew that that moment of pure, unguarded joy, was the best Christmas present of all.

"I'd better get up and go make dinner," Mary said with a regretful sigh a few minutes later.

Carla rose and followed Mary toward the kitchen. She was feeling mellow, undoubtedly from the several glasses of eggnog she had consumed.

"May I help?" she offered.

"Sure." Mary pointed to a colander filled with just-washed potatoes. "Why don't you peel those? That'll give me time to make the hard sauce for the plum pudding. Then all I'll have to do is warm it up in the microwave when we're ready."

Mary pulled out a pan from a cupboard and without bothering to measure or consult a cookbook, threw butter into it. Next she added brown sugar and let the mixture simmer for a bit.

"I've always wanted to be able to cook like that," Carla said, watching her enviously. The sweet smell of the mixture cooking filled the room. "I love to cook, but nothing ever seems to turn out unless I follow the recipe religiously.''

"There's nothing much to it," Mary said, wiping her brow with a hand. She picked up a bottle of brandy and poured a healthy amount into the cooking pot. "All I do is throw some stuff together. Usually it turns out." She grinned as she stirred briskly. "I keep a freezer full of food handy in case of accidents."

Randy stuck his head in the kitchen door. "We've got World War III brewing in the dining room. Drake and Brian are setting the table. Drake wants to use the reindeer tablecloth, but Brian insists it's too faded and tacky."

"I know better than to get in the middle of that one," Mary said with a laugh. She dipped a wooden spoon into the pot and tasted the sauce. "It needs salt." She reached into a cupboard, found the salt, shook a small amount into her palm, then dumped it into the pot. "I'll let them argue that out among themselves. They always have."

Randy grinned and pulled his head out of the doorway.

"You must have had your hands full raising four boys," Carla said.

"It's kept me busy," Mary agreed. Her eyes lit up with amusement. "Young, too. I haven't had time to grow old. But it's been worth it. They've always been good. They've always helped out. Of course, they didn't have much choice with both of us working."

"It must be nice to be a real family." With the point of her knife, Carla picked an eye out of a potato. "That's unusual these days, you know. You're lucky."

"We've worked at it. I've always thought that families are like happiness," Mary said, turning the burner off. "They're a state of mind. They take a lot of care. They take a lot of love."

"There's certainly a lot of care and love in your family," Carla said wistfully.

"Care and love feed on each other," Mary remarked, reaching across the stove to lift a lid on a pot of cooking sweet potatoes. Steam billowed forth as she added, "The more love and care you give, the more you receive."

"I suppose you're right," Carla said slowly. "I never thought of it that way. I see so many kids in my work as a social worker who've never been given a chance to know what happiness or a real family are like."

"Like you," Mary said softly. "I can't imagine you saw much family happiness as a child."

Carla bent her head over the sink, sloughing potato peelings into the kitchen sink. Reference to her own childhood made her feel uncomfortable. She gruffly said, "It wasn't so bad. There were some happy times. Anyway, it was all I knew."

"I remember your first movie," Mary commented, glancing at Carla with watchful eyes. "You were just about Drake's age. I watched you with great interest. You were so pretty and sweet. So innocent."

"That was a long time ago," Carla said, tossing a peeled potato in a large white bowl with unnecessary force. She picked up another potato and added, "Things have changed. I've changed."

"Perhaps." Mary smiled and crossed the room in a few quick steps. Putting an arm around Carla, she gave her a big hug and said, "You're still pretty and sweet."

Carla hugged her back. "But I'm afraid I'm not so innocent anymore."

"No. No one is anymore, I suppose," Mary replied, dropping her arms to her sides. She walked toward the oven. "Tell me, how do you feel about singing again?"

Stabbing the eye of a potato with the point of her knife, Carla said, "I can't say that I'm thrilled to death about it. After all, I wasn't given much choice in the matter."

"Drake told us that he railroaded you." Opening the oven door, Mary pulled a rack out. A delicious-smelling turkey filled a stainless-steel roasting pan. "I can't say I'm surprised. Drake's always been determined when it comes to getting his own way. I guess that comes from being the eldest. He's used to being the boss." Mary pulled the thermometer out of the turkey and squinted at the gauge for a moment. Then she said to Carla, "The turkey's almost done. We'd better get those potatoes started cooking quickly."

Drake's father said the blessing, which was the longest string of words that Carla had heard him utter all day. Then, holding aloft his wineglass until everyone responded in suit, Drake said, "To Carla and Bobby, the newest members of our family. May they find peace and happiness with us."

This was greeted with cheers and laughter, and then it was every man for himself. It was amazing to Carla how fast the mountains of food disappeared from the table. Ham, turkey, mashed potatoes and sweet potatoes all seemed to vanish in the twinkling of an eye.

It took a great deal of effort for Carla to push her chair away from the dinner table an hour later. It took even more effort for her to get up. She couldn't remember ever eating and drinking so much. She'd hardly paid attention to the amount of food she was consuming, so caught up was she in the lighthearted conversation and happy conviviality.

"Now comes the best part of Christmas," Drake said, walking over to her and catching her hand. "Opening the presents."

Carla smiled at him warmly, so full of joy that the brief thought that there wouldn't be any presents under the tree for her didn't bother her at all. Her gift was being welcomed into his family, if only for a short while.

"Are you happy?" Drake asked, winding his arm around her waist. Carla leaned into him and nodded a silent assent.

They strolled into the living room where the Christmas tree sparkled and bedazzled a room basked in dark evening gloom. The firelight cast shadows along one wall and gave off a spicy scent.

"Sit here," Drake instructed, gesturing toward an overstuffed couch parked near the Christmas tree. "I'll be back in a few minutes."

Mary, Henry and Randy followed soon after, and while they talked and laughed, Carla just sat back and relaxed. Someone had put on a Beatles Christmas record this time. Soon the rest of the family had filed into the room. Bobby and Kevin sat on the couch with Carla, while the rest of the family sat cross-legged on the floor.

Everyone but Drake, that is. When Carla heard a raspy voice chanting, "Ho! Ho! Ho!" she turned her head toward the doorway.

"Has everyone been good this year?" Drake greeted, walking into the room. He was wearing a cheap red flannel Santa suit and a shaggy white acrylic beard that wouldn't have fooled a four-year-old. A wide, black plastic belt was strapped tightly over his stomach to prevent the pillow stuffed under his suit from falling.

"No!" the family responded in chorus.

"Good, then I know I have the right house," Drake replied cheerfully, walking toward the tree. "Hmm, I see lots of nice presents here. Anyone want one?"

"Yes!" they all replied.

He leaned over and picked up a gift. "This one says Mom. Do we have a mom in the room?"

Everyone laughed, including Mary, who stuck her hand out to accept the gift. But that wasn't good enough. Drake made her come forward, and she giggled girlishly the whole way.

There were gifts for everyone. Some were jokes, some were serious, and some were overwhelmingly nice.

"This one's for you, Bobby," Drake said, stooping over to pick up a gaily wrapped present in the corner.

"Gee, thanks, Drake," Bobby said, once he had ripped the package open. It was a squat, semiportable antique mahogany Victrola. When Bobby lifted the lid, Carla saw the emblem His Master's Voice and the well-known picture of a dog listening to the giant ear of a gramophone. With the package was a smaller package, full of original 78-RPM records that could be played on the Victrola.

"Wow, Benny Goodman!" Bobby's face lit up with joy. "And Bessie Smith too. Can I play one now?"

"Sure," Drake said as he showed Bobby how to crank up the machine. The record sounded tinny and slightly scratchy, but the magical talents of Benny Goodman could not be denied.

"And here's another present for Bobby," Drake said, looking a trifle puzzled as he picked up a small package. Unlike the rest of the presents, its wrapping was blue and unChristmaslike.

Carla held her breath as Bobby came forward. Accepting the package with a polite thank-you, Bobby opened the card attached to the package. His eyes brightened considerably as he read the words out loud. "Congratulations to you and your new family. Love, Carla."

"I didn't know we were going to be celebrating Christmas," Carla explained, looking embarrassed. "But I brought something for Bobby anyway."

"That was a wonderful thought," Drake said, with glowing eyes fixed firmly on Carla.

Bobby tore apart the small package with excited hands. When he saw what was inside, his voice was jubilant. "Wow! A harmonica. Just what I've been wanting! How did you know? Thanks a lot."

"It once belonged to Tyler Gunther," Carla explained nervously, her hands smoothing a nonexistent wrinkle from her skirt. She added, "Upstairs in my suitcase I've got the papers to document it."

"Thank you, Carla, from both of us," Drake said. Realizing Carla's extreme embarrassment, he walked over to the tree and picked up another package. "This one's for you," he said softly, setting a long box on Carla's lap. "I hope you like it."

"Why, thank you," Carla said, surprised that he had remembered to buy something for her. Carefully, not to tear the pretty Christmas paper, she unwrapped the package. "Oh, how beautiful!"

It was a hurricane lamp, obviously very old and very unusual. The chimney was a pale apricot color and made of thick, double glass. "Thank you, Drake," Carla said softly, running her hand along the raised design of roses on the side of the glass. "But you make me feel so ashamed. I don't have a present for you."

"Would you like to give me a present?" Drake asked.

"Of course," Carla replied.

"Sing 'Remember' for me," was his swift response.

Her hand ceased its stroking of the raised glass as she sucked in her breath. "Remember." Even the thought of that song made her pulse roar, made her heart falter. "Remember" had once been her theme song. It was the final song she'd sung with her mother at that last concert.

"I-I can't," she stammered, trying to find her breath.

"Why not?" he asked, his eyes steady on her. "Don't tell me you've forgotten the words."

"I'll sing you something else, anything else," she said desperately, her hands once more fingering the glass of the lamp. "Any other song but that one."

"I don't want any other song," he said gently. Lifting the lamp out of her hands, he set it on the end table nearby, then pulled her to a standing position in front of him. "I want 'Remember.' Come on, I'll make you a deal. You sing and I'll accompany you on the piano. Okay?"

Carla felt the eyes of the whole family upon her. She felt their love and understanding. She took a deep breath. They had given her so much. It was her turn to give back.

"Okay." She relented, marching over to the corner of the room where the piano stood. Turning toward the family, she leaned against the piano and swallowed nervously, her face chalky white.

With casual unconcern, Drake sauntered across the room and sat down on the piano bench. His studied indifference was all on the surface. Beneath the calm exterior he was as nervous as Carla. Was he doing the right thing in making Carla sing "Remember"? He wanted to push her, but not hurt her or frighten her away.

The room was quiet. All Carla could hear was the furious pumping of her heart. She was going to make a fool of herself. She knew she was.

The strains of piano music pierced the room's silence. She closed her eyes, trying to bring forth the long-forgotten words. When she realized that her mind had gone blank, she felt panic gnawing in the pit of her stomach.

"Easy, Carla," Drake whispered softly. "I know you can do it. Now, show me."

She closed her eyes and let her mind float for a moment. Then the words came to her in a flash. As she waited through the opening refrain, which Drake had already repeated several times, she felt her impatience rising. Then it was time for her to sing.

She felt her blood rush as her voice swelled in song. Her foot tapped a beat and her fingers snapped to the music. The excitement of performing was like a drug to her senses.

She'd always thought that making music with someone was comparable to making love. It took the proper timing, the proper communication, the proper chemistry. She glanced at Drake. His hands flew across the piano keys, but his eyes were watching her. His eyes were loving her. He knew her, he understood her. He'd been right all along, she realized. He did know her better than she knew herself. They were going to make beautiful music together. . . .

Chapter Eight

Carla lay on the bed in her room and looked out through the window to an ink-black, star-studded sky. The stars had never twinkled so brightly back home in Los Angeles, she thought.

She ought to be tired from tossing and turning so much. She ought to be, but she wasn't.

Damn Drake Lanning! Sitting up, she twisted her body and punched angrily at her pillow. A man shouldn't have such charm and good looks. It wasn't fair. It wasn't right. A man shouldn't have such perception. It left a woman with too few defenses.

And that's what she was: defenseless. Giving her pillow another frustrated whack, she turned and settled herself back on the bed.

She hadn't felt so tense and out of control since her mother had died. But here she was, her nerves as tightly coiled as a spring. Throwing back the bed covers, she jumped up and padded barefoot to the window.

Her hands gripped the windowsill, revealing white skin stretched over bony knuckles. Outside, a ribbon of silver moonlight glanced upon the shimmering waters of Lake Arrowhead. Except for the occasional chirping of a frog and the high-pitched whine from the cicadas, all was still. Clean mountain air billowed through the window screens and cooled Carla's face.

A gentle breeze fluttered the yellow corn-silk of her hair. Raising a hand, Carla threaded her fingers underneath the blond strands and lifted her hair away from her shoulders. She felt the breeze tickle the short hairs on her neck.

If only her tension were caused by nervousness about the concert, she mused. That, she could deal with. But it wasn't that at all. Her problem was a lot more basic; a lot more primitive.

She wasn't a naive girl. There'd been men in her life before. But she'd always been careful to choose men she could walk away from. She'd learned long ago that getting emotionally involved with people left you vulnerable and likely to be hurt. And she'd had enough of being hurt for a lifetime. She had no intention of letting it happen again.

But ever since she'd met Drake, her life hadn't been her own. She considered whether he was someone she'd be able to walk away from without regret or sadness. She sighed, knowing the answer to that question.

Look what had happened already. She had vowed to remain cautious around Drake. That had lasted about an hour, and then somehow she'd caught the spirit of Drake's enthusiasm for living. By the time they'd taken their walk together, she'd completely forgotten all the well-intentioned promises she'd made to herself. If Drake hadn't started asking embarrassing questions about the scars on her head she would have let him make love to her.

She sighed again, alternately wishing that she had, and thankful that she hadn't. But if she had . . .

Carla turned around abruptly. A walk. That was what she needed. Some physical exercise might release some of her tension. She walked over to the rocking chair where the lavender silk wrap that matched her nightgown lay discarded in a crumpled heap. Picking it up, she pulled it over her. Then she slipped into matching lavender scuffs.

The only sound she heard as she crept down the stairs was the creaking noise of her weight on the carpeted wooden steps. The front-door hinges squeaked when the door was opened, then she was out in the refreshingly cool darkness of the night.

Without making a conscious decision or knowing why, she headed toward the dock on the lake. A full moon directed the way. Dead leaves crunched and crackled underfoot, and an owl hooted in the distance.

The pier loomed dark and long against the flashing silver and gray water of the lake. Carla stepped onto the dock, her slipper-covered feet making no sound as she padded toward the end of the plankings.

Here was peace, she thought, as she felt a gentle lake breeze ruffle her clothing. For a long moment Carla stood there, looking at the sky, the water and the lights from across the lake. She felt the cool breeze against her skin, and heard the soothing, gentle lapping sound of waves hitting the pilings. Already her nerves were beginning to unwind.

She bent her knees and pulled her negligee underneath her. Then she sat down and let her feet dangle over the edge.

"So, you can't sleep either?" A voice broke the stillness. It was low and husky and seemed to float across the dark water.

Carla realized with a start that she wasn't surprised to hear Drake's voice. She'd hoped he'd be there. No, she'd known he'd be here. Wasn't that why she'd come? She turned and looked for him, but all she saw was the shadow of tall pines against the glitter-dotted black sky.

"I wanted to ask you to come to my cabin tonight," he said. The huskiness of his voice drifted and echoed over the water. "But I knew it wasn't the right time to ask you, with the whole family standing around. It's better this way, don't you think? More romantic. More spontaneous."

A slow burn started in Carla. He seemed to be taking a lot for granted. The knowledge that she'd come with the subconscious hope of finding him infuriated her even more. She rose and said, "I never talk to people I can't see. And since I can't see you, I'm going back inside."

She'd only taken a few steps before a tall figure appeared in front of her. She looked up. Moonlight illuminated the harshly rugged contours of his face. His amber eyes were as dark and as impenetrable as obsidian. She found his stare unnerving. Taking in a deep breath, she drew her eyes downward. She saw a bare chest, taut and smooth with bronze skin and a sprinkling of dark, wiry hair. Tight, low-slung blue jeans covered his long, muscular legs. He wore no shoes.

"I'm here," he said as his hands cupped the nape of her neck. Her eyes flickered up again. "I assure you I'm all flesh and blood. Would you like me to show you?"

"I'm tired," Carla replied, the tension she'd felt all day suddenly snapping. "I don't have the energy for your games. I don't have the patience. I'm going back to the house."

"I'm tired, too," Drake said, his voice low and throaty as he wound his arms tightly around her. A hand reached out and tenderly stroked her hair. "Tired of all the lies. Tired of all this dillydallying. Come with me, Carla. Let me love you. I need you. I want you. I've tried to be patient, but I've already waited too long."

She felt the leashed force in him, seething like a volcano ready to erupt. She felt fear—of herself and of him. His power was too strong. She might never be free again if she let it consume her. She lashed out defensively. "You say you want me, that you need me. But for what? For how long? I'm not one of your rock 'n' roll groupies, you know."

"Did you think I thought you were?" he demanded, as he pulled her head around to him.

"I don't know what you think," Carla replied raggedly. She shoved her hands against his chest in an effort to get away, but he was too strong for her.

"But you know I want you," he said harshly, dipping his head to her ear. She felt the heat of his breath and the fierce, seductive swath of his tongue branding a trail.

"Yes, I know that you want me," Carla whispered. She took in a deep breath, annoyed at the way her emotions were beginning to betray her. She felt a pulse rat-a-tat-tat at her throat, then felt it amplify throughout her body. "But why? For how long? Your attention span with women isn't known for its longevity."

"I've never cared for a woman as I care for you." His mouth blazed a path from her ear to her lips. "I've never wanted a woman as I want you."

Carla tried turning her head away, but he turned her face back toward him. Then she felt the touch of his lips on hers, caressing her.

Molten fire flowed into her. The blood in her limbs heated and thickened. Long-dormant passion spewed forth from the deepest, most secret and primitive regions of her body. And then there were no more doubts.

Drake felt Carla tremble against him. Was she afraid? He'd have to show her that love didn't destroy; it created. He'd make her believe it.

His hands slipped underneath the silken wrapper and he lovingly stroked the rounded contours of her body. He'd known how she'd feel beneath his fingers.

"Oh, Carla," he breathed, as one of his hands slid under her bottom. The other curved over her shoulder. Then, with one effortless movement, he lifted her. She nestled her head against his chest as she watched the stars overhead swim woozily. Around them, the trees towered like silent, lumbering giants of the night. The wind rustled the branches of a tree nearby. She felt safe—for the first time in her life—in the comfort of his arms.

Although Drake's breathing was shallow and hoarse as he carried her to his cabin, it wasn't from physical exertion. His bare feet hardly made a sound as they hit the wooden planking of the pier. Then they were on the path, following the narrow, rocky trail to his cabin.

Carla rested her head against him and mused. Agreeing to do the concert had wrought changes in her life. Making love with Drake would explode that life into a million tiny pieces.

Yet she knew that making love with him was inevitable. If it didn't happen tonight, it would happen another night. The attraction, the chemistry between them, was too strong to deny. It was just a matter of time. And she wanted it to happen tonight.

Only a dim light shone through the windows as Drake climbed the cabin steps. The screen door groaned as he opened it and carried her across the threshold. Then they were passing through the living room and toward the bedroom. Gently, Drake deposited her on the bed.

Carla felt bereft as he crossed the room away from her. Stifling an urge to call him back to her, she looked around. The room was comfortable rather than glamorous. She was sitting on a king-size bed that overlooked a picture window. Through the screens she could see the moonlight-dazzled water of Lake Arrowhead, with its softly capping silver-and-pewter waves. Across the lake, on the opposite shore, gleamed a smattering of lights.

Drake strode over to a mirrored chest of drawers and proceeded to light a kerosene lantern. He removed the clear glass chimney and then picked up a book of matches that lay nearby. With one quick stroke, both match and wick were ignited and a flame began to glow.

Carla looked at Drake, who was replacing the chimney on the lantern. She remarked quietly, "You're very sure of yourself, aren't you?"

He turned to look at her, his head tilted questioningly. "What do you mean?"

"You headed straight for the bedroom. You didn't even make a pretense of stopping in the living room," Carla said. Her hands fidgeted with the seam on the quilt beneath her.

"I don't like pretenses," Drake replied quietly. Slowly, like an omnipotent and primeval god, he walked toward the bed. The wavering lantern light cast a dull-orange glow over the tanned, tightly roped muscles of his body. The tight blue jeans he wore emphasized his masculinity instead of hiding it. "I've always thought pretenses were a waste of both time and energy."

"Then I guess you think good manners are a waste of time, too," Carla said, lowering her eyes to the quilt and crossing her arms over her chest. The time for turning back had long passed, but suddenly she felt shy and unsure. Would he be able to see through to her insecurity?

"There's nothing wrong with good manners if it prevents hurting people's feelings," Drake replied. The bedsprings creaked as he sat down. He looked at her for a long moment, noticing the way her arms were wrapped protectively across her breasts and the way she refused to look him in the eye. He said softly, "Is that what's wrong? Have I somehow hurt your feelings? Or is it just a case of cold feet?"

Carla raised her eyes to the ceiling and watched the flickering light dance among shadows. In a tight, strained voice, she replied, "I don't know what's wrong. I just know I'm scared."

"There's nothing to be scared of. I won't hurt you. And I won't rush you, either. I promise." He'd promised he'd be patient, but seeing her on his bed in the lavender and lace negligee almost drove all thought from his brain. He could see the outline of the darkened peaks of her nipples under the thin silk. And her skin gleamed like ivory satin. To be so close and to lose her now was more than he could endure. But he wanted her soul, not just her body. He added gently, "I'm sorry if I came on too strong. I guess it's a defect in my character. Perhaps you'd better go now."

"No." The force with which she pronounced these words echoed loudly in the small room and startled them both. She added, "Just give me some more time. I'll be okay."

He tried to concentrate on looking at just her face. He saw the glint of her blond hair in the moonlight and the sharp outline of her pale cheekbone. Her eyelids fluttered nervously. A pulse beat erratically in her throat. He leaned closer and murmured, "You shouldn't be surprised at my lack of manners. I thought you'd decided that I don't have any."

"That's true," she agreed. She felt her tension ease as the atmosphere between them lightened. She said with nervous gaiety, "Anyway, who cares? I'm sure Emily Post never wrote a chapter on bedroom manners."

Drake leaned over and held his face next to Carla's. He was so close that she could see the stubble of his beard and beads of sweat on his brow. Carla breathed in the musky male smell of him. As if making a choice, she reached out a hand and gently stroked his arm. She felt the brush of hair and the warmth of his skin beneath her fingers.

"Careful, Carla," Drake said in a hoarse voice. "Go easy on me. I'm not made of iron."

"What are you made of?" she asked teasingly. Suddenly everything was fine. He'd been gentle and undemanding when she'd needed it. He'd understood her hesitation. She leaned over and planted her lips on his for a brief, exploratory kiss. The bristle of his beard scratched her chin as she said, "I think my time's up, Drake. I'm okay now."

His hand slid over the smooth silk of her body and gently roamed, learning its curves and softness. His amber eyes bore into her as he said huskily, "Are you sure?"

"I'm sure," she replied, kissing him again.

"You're so beautiful," he murmured.

Men had said that to Carla before, but she'd never really felt beautiful. Not until now. Not until this moment.

The shadowy light from the lantern cast a dull, rosy glow over their tightly meshed bodies. Drake made love to her slowly, savoring the nectar of her body. She was a rare flower unfolding, blossoming into fragrant beauty just for him.

Lips that were tender and patient lingered over the lavender silk and lace that covered her breasts. Gently his teeth nudged the fabric down until first one, and then another breast, was exposed.

His hands caressed her until Carla felt her nipples grow hard and taut with desire. His mouth traveled up to her lips and playfully nibbled around their outline. Her tongue flicked out to meet his, eventually drawing it into the moist recesses of her mouth.

She was aware of him everywhere. She felt his hand swiftly removing the silken fabric of her nightgown and his jean-clad legs rubbing against the satiny smoothness of hers.

Suddenly she wanted no barriers between them. She tugged at the snap of his jeans and she heard the rip of his zipper as it came unfastened. Then he lifted himself so that she could pull off his jeans and briefs in one long, fluid motion.

She let out a sigh of pure pleasure when their naked bodies finally found each other. Carla rotated her hips against his, arching to find the fulfillment only he could bring.

Drake found the essence of her femininity and began to gently caress her. Carla writhed and twisted until finally she could take no more. "Now, Drake. Please..."

"It's too soon," Drake murmured, his lips trailing up to her ears.

"Now, Drake," she begged, taking him into her hands. Her fingers began to weave a sensual magic. Drake shuddered and closed his eyes, then opened them and gazed deeply into hers.

"Look at me Carla," he urged. "I want you to remember this moment forever."

She opened frantic, passion-filled eyes as her hands groped desperately for him. "Now, Drake," she pleaded. "Now!"

He entered her as smoothly as silk gliding over soft skin. She let out a happy, ecstatic cry. He was deep within her, all his energy and drive throbbing into every cell of her body.

She slid her hands over his perspiration-slick skin. She liked the feel of his rippling muscles under her touch. Her hands glided down to his buttocks and felt undulations as he moved back and forth, pulsing an intimate, erotic rhythm.

She was gasping for breath, stunned by the fusion that consumed her. Shimmering waves grew and grew, and finally she felt a violent explosion rip her apart. Fragmented, she was reeling in space, a dark unlimited space that knew no beginning and no ending. Then, as she drifted back, she knew with a joyous certainty that she'd never been so complete or so fulfilled in all her life.

The aroma of bacon frying and coffee brewing assaulted Carla's senses. For an instant she was confused. Where was she? She looked around her, noting the sun-dappled bedroom with its view of the lake. Then she remembered.

Last night. And, oh, what a night it had been. Every time she'd thought she had no more love to give, Drake had shown her she was wrong. A lingering kiss, a stroke of her thighs—that's all it had taken for him to ignite her passion once again. The sun was tinting the sky a pale-rose color when exhaustion had finally claimed them. But even a well-deserved rest couldn't separate them. They'd gone to sleep with their bodies entwined.

As Carla yawned and stretched, she felt the protest of muscles she'd long ignored screaming from overuse. Pulling back the covers, she hopped out of bed, feeling remarkably chipper despite her lack of sleep.

A large T-shirt lay discarded on a chair next to the dresser. She picked it up and pulled it on.

"Good morning, beautiful," Drake greeted, turning his head toward her as she shuffled into the kitchen. His eyes looked pleased with the way the T-shirt fell over her breasts and skimmed the tops of her thighs. Carla thought he looked equally devastating in a pair of tight jean cutoffs. "That's a stunning outfit you have on," he said.

"Thank you," Carla replied. "And good morning. I like your outfit, too."

"It's great until the bacon spatters," he said with a grin. With an expert flick of a wrist, Drake cracked an egg on the side of the black cast-iron skillet and added, "How do you like your eggs?"

"Over easy."

"Just like I like my women."

Carla raised a mocking eyebrow and smiled back. "Really? I could have sworn you liked them sunny-side up."

"I think this topic is too raw a yolk for this early in the morning," Drake said, with a straight face. "How about some coffee?"

"Please," Carla said placidly, unwilling to give Drake any satisfaction by groaning at such a terrible pun. She stretched her arms and stifled a big yawn with her hand.

"Cream and sugar?" Drake asked, picking up the glass coffee maker and pouring her a cup.

"Just cream, please." Carla accepted the cup with a smile and sat down at the kitchen table. A navy-blue and rust linen tablecloth covered the table. Neatly set on it were matching napkins, silverware and rust-colored stoneware plates. A kerosene lamp was placed in the center, giving off more scent than light. Carla sniffed the air, trying to decide whether the scent was bayberry or strawberry. "If you're trying to impress me with your domestic abilities, you're doing a good job. Breakfast has always been one of those meals that I could never summon the courage to tackle."

"I once worked as a short-order cook. The doors opened at 6:00 a.m.," Drake said, lifting the lid of another skillet on the stove. Steam rose from the pan as he put the lid on a nearby counter. "Breakfast is ready."

Carla put down her coffee cup. "Good, I'm starving."

"But first I need my tip," Drake said, walking over to her. He caught her hand, pulled her up from the chair and wrapped his arms tightly around her body.

"You don't get a tip until after breakfast," Carla protested with a laugh. Nevertheless, she threw her arms around his neck and raised her head for his kiss.

He was gentle, ever so gentle when he kissed her. But still she felt the fire start to rage.

"We're going to starve at this rate," Drake said huskily, lifting his head to look deep into her blue eyes. "How about another tip after breakfast?"

"Okay," Carla murmured breathlessly. "That sounds like a good idea to me."

She never ate breakfast at home, but this morning she ate two eggs, five pieces of bacon, and the biggest mound of cottage-fried potatoes this side of Mount Whitney. She finished her second cup of coffee, then pushed her plate away, saying, "I guess it's time for me to do the dishes now."

"What? I don't get my tip?" Drake asked.

Carla made a face. "I ate too much. How about a rain check?"

"I don't know about that," Drake countered. Folding his hands behind his neck, he tilted his chair and leaned back, his long legs stretched out straight in front of him. "It's summer. That's the dry season for L.A. It might be a long time before it rains."

"You're right," Carla said, stacking the silverware on the plates. She shoved back her chair and rose, plates in hand. Turning, she gave him a lopsided grin, "It might be at least half an hour."

"Practically forever," Drake replied, shaking his head sadly. "If it's going to take that long, why don't I go back to the house and pack your bags?"

"Pack my bags," Carla repeated. "Whatever do you need to do that for?"

Drake tried to stifle a smile. "Were you intending on showing up in that?" He gestured at the T-shirt she was wearing. "Or last night's negligee perhaps?"

"Oh, that," Carla said, pursing her lips. "Well, I suppose you could pick me up a few things. But I don't need a whole bag."

"Yes, you do," Drake said. "You're staying here with me from now—"

The look in her eyes stopped him. "Wait a minute," she said uneasily. "I don't recall agreeing to that."

"I took it for granted," Drake replied, looking bewildered. "Surely you don't plan to sneak up here every night. It doesn't make sense. It's impractical."

Her voice was tight when she replied, "Look, last night was wonderful. But I'm not sure I want to move in with you. I've already told you, I'm not one of your groupies. If you're looking for a live-in girlfriend and some quick action on the side, you've come to the wrong woman."

With that, she stalked out of the kitchen.

Chapter Nine

Would you mind telling me what this is all about?"
Drake demanded, leaning an arm against the jamb of
the bedroom door. His tall, solid frame filled the
doorway as he watched Carla march determinedly toward the closet and wrench the louvered door open.
Her hands shuffled frantically through the hangers.

"What does it look like? I'm searching for something to wear so I can get out of here," Carla replied.
She pulled out a blue plastic rain poncho from the
closet and slammed the door shut with a vengeance.
She spun on her heels and faced him, adding, "And
this will suit my purposes just fine."

"Carla, calm down," Drake urged her, crossing the
room. As Carla unhooked the poncho from its hanger

with trembling fingers, he rested light hands on the backs of her shoulders and began to knead gently as he implored. "Please don't go storming out of here without our talking things over first."

"What's there to talk about? You've got everything all decided." She twisted away from him and then slipped the poncho over her head. The blue plastic material slithered and swished and then hit the floor. The poncho was far too long for her. She looked ridiculous—like a child dressed up in her mother's clothing—but Drake knew better than to laugh at her.

"After all, I'm nobody special," she continued. "Just another woman. I suppose your family must be used to seeing you shack up with a new woman every weekend by now."

"So that's what this is all about," Drake said, dragging a hand through his curly brown hair. Shoving his hands into his jeans pockets, he said, "Look, I'm sorry if I've upset you. But you've got me all wrong. You're not just any girl to me. You're different. I've never brought a woman here before."

"Hah," Carla scoffed. She glared at him. "You don't really expect me to believe that, do you? I know what you're like. I know your reputation. I've even met Angie. And have you forgotten what you told me in your interview? Quote: 'I like a woman in my life. I like a woman in my bed.' End quote."

Drake muttered an oath under his breath and then said, "I was angry and defensive. I was trying to rile you, Carla. I'm not saying I've been an angel—far from it—but I'm not totally irresponsible, either. And

Angie... Angie and I have an understanding. She's been there when I needed her, and vice versa, but there's never been anything more. She's been a friend. I promise that you're the first woman I've ever brought here.

"What do you think I am? For God's sake, Carla, this is my parents' place. I wouldn't bring just anybody here. You've met my parents. You know what they're like. What I do in my home may be my own private business, but my mother would never go for my bringing a different girl up here every weekend and flaunting it in her face. My whole family knows you're someone special. Don't you?"

Carla lowered her eyes and said quietly, "No."

She felt the grip of his strong hands on her shoulders as he pulled her into his arms. She heard the pounding of his heart and the ragged pace of his breathing. His callused fingers lifted her chin so he could look deep into her eyes. She saw the rough texture of his lined, deeply tanned skin and the thick fringe of dark lashes that framed his amber eyes. He said softly, "You are special, believe me. Don't ever, not for even a second, think you're not. You've turned my world around. When I look back at all those years when I refused to get involved emotionally, when I had a new girl for every day and week, I now understand why I couldn't get involved. I was looking for you, Carla. I was waiting for you. All my life I've been waiting for you. I must have you and only you in my life—for now, and forever. Otherwise I'm lost. I wish I could make you believe that."

Their eyes locked and for a moment she did believe him. She felt the force of his personality pulling her toward him like a magnet. Swallowing to relieve the dry, strangling tightness in her throat, she said shakily, "Even if I did believe it, I wouldn't move in with you."

His eyes narrowed and darkened. "Why not?"

"Your whole family would know we were sleeping together. How could I face them? What would they think? I came here to work, to practice for a concert. I didn't come here to be your bed partner."

"They're adults," Drake said confidently. "They'd understand."

"Maybe they would understand," Carla agreed slowly. "But what kind of an example would that set for Bobby? How would he feel if he knew that I was sleeping with you? He's known me for years; I've been an authority figure to him. And would he be able to accept me as your...woman...knowing that I turned down your original application because of your—" she hesitated and then couldn't help grinning "—active social life. It would make me look like an incredible hypocrite if I then began to flaunt my relationship with you."

"You see what happens when you set yourself up as a judge and jury on morals," Drake said, his eyes glittering mockingly. "You get caught in a trap of your own making."

"I wasn't setting myself up as a judge and jury on morals," Carla defended. "I was doing my job. I was doing what I thought was right. And I'd do the same again. I still think I was right. That's just my point: I don't think someone Bobby's age should have to watch while adults play musical beds. It's too unsettling for them."

"Are you speaking from experience?"

She squashed down unpleasant childhood memories of stilted conversations with her mother and strange men over breakfast and glared at him, annoyed that he had hit so close to home; that he knew her so well. "Yes, I am, as a matter of fact."

"Okay, I'll be reasonable and admit you might have a point," Drake conceded. He looked at her with assessing eyes for a long moment and then added quietly, "But I have an easy solution. Why don't we get married?"

"Married!" Carla echoed in a startled voice. Of all possible things, that was the last thing she'd expected him to say.

"Yeah, married," he said, grinning casually. His eyes weren't a bit casual. They were dark and intense. "You know the routine. To have and to hold until death do us part. Shoes and rice and everything nice."

Carla caught her breath. "If this a joke, I don't think it's very funny."

"It's not a joke," Drake said, reaching out a hand and cupping her chin so he could look into her eyes. "I've never been more serious in my life."

"But we hardly know one another," Carla objected, flustered. "We—"

"I feel I've known you all my life," he interrupted, spreading his fingers and gently massaging her. She felt her pulse begin to jump as her muscles tensed and then relaxed beneath his agile, knowing hands. "And I'm sure I must have known you in a couple of lives before this one, too."

"I didn't know you believed in reincarnation," Carla said, a trifle breathlessly.

"Neither did I until I met you," he said, his voice low and beguiling. He dropped his head and nuzzled his lips against her temple and her hair.

She thought it sounded like a wonderful idea as she savored the heat of his breath in her hair. The scent of him, redolent of male musk and woodsy cologne engulfed her. The touch of him, warm and always giving, overwhelmed her. She raised her lips for his kiss and pictured herself loving and living with him for the rest of her life. Oh, what a fairy-tale romance it would make. How happy Drake's family would be. Maybe they could even give Mary that longed-for grandchild. The reporters would eat up such a fairy-tale romance. The story would even manage to eclipse the amount of publicity she'd received when her mother had died.

The story would even manage to eclipse the amount of publicity she'd received when her mother had died.

She felt her heart suddenly quiver and shake as she remembered how the press had acted that time. They'd been a pack of wild, hungry dogs and she'd been the only bone for a hundred miles around. They had snarled and probed and fought; if Dr. Cook hadn't lied for her, she never would have made it through that difficult time without a complete nervous breakdown.

Marrying Drake would bring it all back—the reporters, the limelight, the questions she would never be able to answer truthfully. Carla shuddered and reluctantly broke away from him. "It would never work," she said, taking a step backward. With considerable effort, she managed to jerk her mind back to the hard, cruel reality of life instead of dreams.

"Why not?" he demanded, reaching out a hand and pulling her back to him.

"Because I'm Carla Foster," she explained. "Because you're Drake Lanning. Because I vowed ten years ago that I would never have anything to do with show business again."

"So we come back to that again?" he said wearily, dropping his hands and stepping away from her. "When are you ever going to learn not to be afraid?"

"Probably never," Carla said, wishing she could reach out and touch him once again. She felt bereft and alone, as though part of her was dying. Which it probably was. Her voice cracked as she said, "I'm sorry. I can't help who and what I am. Believe me, I wish I could."

"You're sorry," he repeated, his voice suddenly as cold and brittle as ice. She'd seen him angry before, but this was much worse. He looked violent. "Sorry. Yes, I guess that's a good word to describe this whole thing." He thrust his hands into his jeans pockets and balled them into fists, adding, "Tell me, Carla, what was last night? Just a casual romp? I thought that was supposed to be my style, not yours."

She wanted to tell him that last night had meant everything to her, that she'd never cared for a man as she did for him; that she'd never forget him. But the words wouldn't come. In a tone that managed to surprise even Carla by it mildness, she said, "You're an attractive man. I suppose any woman would find you hard to resist."

"I see." He pulled a hand out of his pocket and raised it to her chin, jerking her head toward him so he could look once again into her eyes. "I can't help wondering. If I were Drake Lanning the plumber or Drake Lanning the lawyer instead of Drake Lanning the musician, would I be more acceptable?"

A moment passed and then another, but still she said nothing. What was there to say? His searching eyes had already penetrated her soul and found her answer. "You little fool," he uttered, wrenching his hand from her chin as if it were a hot iron. "So you're going to throw it all away—a chance for love and the brass ring, a chance of a lifetime." His voice was husky and threatening. "Tell me, Carla. Are you a liar as well as a coward? I want to hear you say you don't love me. I want to hear you say you don't care. Tell me. I want to hear it from your lips."

"I don't care. I don't love you," she whispered. "I don't love you, really I don't."

He gripped her arm tightly. "What happened all those years ago to make you so scared? I know you were close to your mother. I know it must have been a terrible shock to lose her the way you did. But there's got to be more to the story than that."

"I don't want to talk about it," she said as she felt her stomach go hollow and plummet to her feet. With a trembling voice, she said, "Let go of me. You're hurting me. You have no right to keep me here."

"Only the right of someone who's loved and lost," Drake replied roughly, his voice brutal from disappointment and pain. "I figure that gives me some rights. And I do want to talk about it. And we're going to if I have to keep you here all day."

All the loneliness and pain of those years came tumbling down on her. She felt angry at him for reminding her of it, and angry at herself for allowing it still to hurt. "So you want to hear the whole story, do you?" she spat out. "You think you're tough. You think you know everything, don't you?" She jerked her arm away and faced him defiantly, hands on her hips. Her blue eyes flashed as cold and hard and dark as sapphires. "You think I was close to my mother. You think we had a loving relationship. God, how I wish it were so. The truth is she hated me. She did everything she could to make my life a living hell. The best thing that ever happened to me was the night she fell over that railing."

Drake stood still, watching her, saying nothing as Carla slowly paced up and down the room. The blue poncho covering her was suffocating her body, so she angrily wrenched it over her head and discarded it onto the floor. Then she turned her head and tossed him a bitter smile as she said, "I can see the surprise on your face. You thought, like everyone else did, that she loved me. After all, we were the much publicized mother-daughter team. We made all those lovey-dovey movies together."

Carla unconsciously rubbed her arms. "As a child I could never understand why she hated me so much. I wasn't a bad or ugly child. And I tried hard to please her. But nothing ever seemed to work. Oh, she'd play the proud and pleased mother in public, of course. But the minute we were alone I'd hear in minute detail everything I'd done wrong."

She walked over to the window and stared sightlessly at the sparkling blue waters of Lake Arrowhead. Her face was averted, her back to Drake as she said in a faraway voice, "My mother's career had begun to falter when we made our first movie together when I was three. The movie became a smash hit and reestablished her popularity. But there was one big problem: the few times the studio gave her scripts without me, the movies were a flop. After a couple of these failures, the studio insisted on giving her scripts that included a part for me. I know my mother greatly resented this. She was a very competitive woman and she always considered me her major competition."

Whirling around, she faced him. "And so we lived a lie. In public and on the screen we were the best of friends. In private we were the bitterest of enemies. I've heard people say what a shame it was that my mother never received an Oscar; she was such a marvelous actress; she really deserved one. I'll have to agree that truer words were never spoken. Mother was a marvelous actress. She managed to fool the whole world. I grew up hearing people tell me how lucky I was: my mother wasn't like most screen mothers; she really cared about me; she took time with me; and wasn't it sweet. We even dressed in look-alike mother-daughter dresses."

She began to laugh, a long, chillingly harsh laugh. "I always wanted to correct them, to tell them the truth, but I knew I didn't dare. And maybe they were right, after all. Mother wasn't like most screen mothers; she was far, far worse. She was a monster, in fact."

She began to pace the room once again as she tried to marshal her tormented thoughts. She felt her heart tripping fast and loud, like a machine gun spewing pain and fear.

She came to a halt in front of the window again. Outside the sky was blue, the sun a golden ball hanging amid frothy white cumulus clouds. It was a beautiful summer day, much like another beautiful summer day many years ago: her eighth birthday. Raising her arm, her fingers began to probe at her scalp until they found the long, jagged place where her hair wouldn't grow. She turned to Drake and demanded, "Do you remember asking me about this scar on my head?"

He was standing just a few feet away from her. Nodding, he remained silent, his dark eyes intent upon her.

"I told you that I fell from my bicycle. It was a lie, of course. Battered children often lie to protect their parents. I should know; my mother used to beat me all the time."

She felt her knees begin to quiver and her stomach start to heave. She sat down on the bed. When she spoke, her voice was a high-pitched, cracked monotone. "I received this scar on my eighth birthday. Mother had decked us out in our usual mother-daughter dresses and invited the press and a few friends to my birthday party. I remember being especially excited. You see, children were going to be invited to this party. Except for when I was at school, I wasn't allowed to play with other children. Mother felt I'd learn nasty habits from them. Children have a habit of getting dirty and mother hated dirt.

"The press being there didn't faze me. I was accustomed to them by then. Mother always invited the press when she had a party for me. I used to think the word *press* came from the word *impress* because Mother always did her best to impress them when they were around."

She stopped to collect her thoughts as her hand nervously fingered the scar on her scalp. "Mother was busy talking to the press, so we kids decided to play hide-and-seek. I was determined not to be found and so I climbed up a tree. And then I ripped my dress." She twisted her head to look up at him. "That's not a very serious crime for an eight-year-old do you think? A torn dress? After all, I had plenty of other dresses, all bought by the studio. One dress shouldn't have mattered very much. Well, let me tell you, I knew better. I spent the rest of the party hiding from my

mother. I knew once she saw the torn dress, I was in
for it.

"When everyone had left, I tried to sneak away and
change without my mother seeing me." She shook her
head ruefully. "I don't know why I thought I could get
away with that. I should have known better. Or perhaps I was just trying to put off the inevitable for as
long as possible. Anyway, my mother caught me
sneaking up the stairs. She'd had too much to drink
and she was already in a lousy mood. When she saw
the torn dress she went wild. She grabbed me by the
arm and told me spanking was too good for me; that
I was a wicked, evil child. Then she pulled off one of
her shoes—a gold lamé spiked high heel—and began
to hit me over the head with it." Carla flinched, remembering the pain and terror as if it were yesterday.
"Mother hit me until my head began to ring with pain.
I cried and pleaded with her to stop but she
wouldn't...or couldn't. I tried to get away but she was
stronger than me. She kept on beating me and beating me."

Covering her face with her hands, Carla let out a
muffled sob and then continued, her voice breaking
with emotion. "I must have eventually passed out because when I awoke she was gone. I was lying on the
floor and there was blood all around me. I can still
remember the salty taste of blood in my mouth. My
God, there was a lot of blood. It took me hours to get
that matted, sticky mess of blood out of my hair."

"Go on. Let it out," Drake urged softly, kneeling
in front of her and resting his hands on her shoulder.

"Let it all out. It's been festering inside of you for too long."

"Music was my way of escaping. When I was busy playing or singing I could forget about the violence and pain. The world was a happy and beautiful place. I was glad to be alive. Best of all, Mother approved of my interest in music. It was something I could do that I didn't get punished for. You see, music didn't get me dirty. And since she was also a musician, my musical talent was a reflection on her.

"Still, the beatings continued. I learned to sublimate the pain by singing silently to myself. That worked for quite a while until one day I made a mistake. I sang the song out loud while my mother was hitting me. She went into a rage and knocked me halfway across the room. I fell against the cocktail table and broke my arm."

Tears misted her eyes and, looking down at him, she smiled ruefully. His hands tightened reassuringly on her shoulders. "I don't know why I'm crying. That broken arm was a blessing in disguise. The doctor asked my mother a lot of embarrassing questions about how I'd gotten the broken arm and bruises. After that she was careful not to leave any marks."

"Wasn't there anyone to help you? Anyone you could tell?" Drake asked, taking her cold, lifeless hands in his hands. He rubbed her hands gently, trying to knead warmth back into them. "A servant? A teacher? A relative?"

"The servants were all illegal immigrants from Mexico, cheap to hire and afraid to get involved. Once

I tried telling one of my teachers. I guess I was about twelve at the time. Mother accused me of lying and everyone believed her. When she got me home afterward she told me that if I ever said a word against her again, she'd kill me. Knowing my mother and her temper, I believed her."

"Oh, Carla, I wish I'd been there to help," Drake said, tightening his grip on her hands.

"I wish you'd been there, too." Carla sobbed against his bare chest. She felt the prickle of his wiry chest hairs against her nose and cheek. Tightening her grip on his forearms, she felt reassured by the strength and firmness of his muscles. "But it wouldn't have mattered. Nobody could help. It was just something I had to live through."

"After hearing about your childhood I can understand why you're afraid to get involved with me," Drake said, slipping his arms around her back and gathering her close to him. "But that was a long time ago. It's all in the past. Won't you trust me? Won't you give me a chance? You must know that I would never do anything to hurt you. I love you too much. That's why I'm asking you to share my life with me."

Reluctantly, she pushed him away from her. Looking deep into his eyes, she tried to read the answer to her question before she'd even asked it. She smiled tremulously. "You say you love me. You say you want to share your life with me. But I haven't finished my story. And quite frankly, I'm afraid to. Are you sure you want to hear what happened the night my mother died? You may hate me after I've told you."

He squeezed her fingers to reassure her. "I love you, Carla. I could never hate you. Tell me what happened that night. I want to know."

She sighed and bit her lip. This was her deepest, most terrible secret. It had tormented her for years. When she told him this, he'd know everything there was to know about her. She'd be stripped, defenseless. A muscle tightened in her jaw. "All right. I'll tell you the whole truth and nothing but. But you can never, ever repeat what happened that night to another living soul. Do you promise?"

"With all my heart, Carla," Drake said, stroking her small hands with his large ones. "You should know by now that I would never do anything to hurt you."

"Hurting me isn't the problem," Carla warned. "You would also hurt someone else—someone who lied to protect me. That's why I've never told anyone what really happened that night."

"Tell me, Carla. Trust me," Drake replied. "I love you. I need to know."

Carla took a deep breath. "My mother didn't fall over that railing by accident. I pushed her. I suppose that makes me a murderer, but I've never regretted it—not for one single minute of my life." As she felt his fingers around hers suddenly grow limp from shock, Carla gently extricated her hands. With sad, teary eyes, she added, "Now, look at me face-to-face. Tell me once again how much you love me."

Chapter Ten

The room was silent. All Carla could hear was the loud hammering sound of her heart. She watched Drake's eyes widen with surprise at her words. When he remained quiet for what seemed like an eternity to her, she knew she'd lost him.

"I warned you not to prod," she said quietly. She felt numb, as if all emotion had been drained out of her. She added in a wooden voice, "But you wouldn't listen. You had to know the truth. Now aren't you sorry you asked?" Wrenching away from him, she got up from the bed and walked over to the window. "You see, I was right. You loved a dream, Drake—not the real me. Now that you know what I really am, you don't love me anymore. That's not surprising. I always knew you couldn't. How could anyone love a murderer?''

She remained standing by the window, her eyes wide and staring, not hearing or seeing anything. She was oblivious when Drake rose and swiftly crossed the room to her. Even the feel of his strong hands taking hold of her shoulders managed to penetrate her consciousness only vaguely.

"I don't believe it. You're no more a murderer than I am," he said, taking her in his arms. His lips planted quick kisses in her hair and along the scar on her scalp. "Your mother was a monster. She pushed you too far. I'll bet you anything it was self-defense. But your conscience won't let you admit it, not even to yourself."

"Some people would call it self-defense," she replied wearily. "But that would be whitewashing the truth. I pushed her. I wanted her dead. I was glad when she died. It was the best thing that ever happened to me."

"Tell me what happened," Drake asked, holding her tightly. "Tell me exactly what happened."

"We got home from the concert late that night," she said, gently extricating herself from his arms and stepping aside. She needed distance, she needed concentration to tell her story. Her face was pale, and her voice was very low. "It must have been about twelve o'clock. I can still picture us walking up that winding staircase to our bedrooms. My mother was wearing royal-blue satin and I was in white eyelet and pink ribbons. The dress I'd worn that night was far too unsophisticated for an eighteen-year-old, and I had put up a fuss about wearing it. Not that it'd done any good. Mother had insisted I wear it anyway. Despite plastic surgery and a rigorous diet, she was beginning to show her age. Having a grown-up daughter was too much of a reminder for her to bear.

"The phone began to ring as we went upstairs. Mother, who was expecting a call from one of her boyfriends, hurried up to the second-floor landing to answer it. At first she sounded happy. I gathered from her end of the conversation that it was the director, Jason Mather, telephoning about a part in a movie. I heard Mother say she'd love to do the part. She was silent for a bit as he talked and then suddenly she flared up and began shouting. I was in my bedroom by then but I could hear her yelling at him from there.

"Mather had offered the part to me instead of her and she was furious. I heard the phone slam in its cradle and then Mother was calling for me to come to her immediately. I thought about refusing and locking my door instead, but I knew from previous experience that putting off a quarrel would just make her angrier."

Carla was breathing faster. Her eyes were fixed on the blank white ceiling, seeing another place, another time. As tears began to course down her cheeks, Drake reached out a finger and gently wiped them away. She was oblivious to his touch, oblivious to anything but the past. In a choked voice, she continued. "I came out of my room slowly, frightened but not wanting to show it. And there she was. I can still see her standing by the telephone table in her vivid-blue dress and heavy makeup. As I walked toward her, I told myself not to be cowardly or afraid. I remember noticing the wrinkles on her face and the way her skin sagged on her upper arms. Getting old must be difficult for her, I thought. I reminded myself to be patient and understanding.

"We had one of those typical Hollywood grand-mansion kind of homes with a landing that looked onto a huge crystal chandelier overhead and a marble-floored foyer below. The telephone stand was just a few feet from the railing. As I walked toward Mother, she began to scream at me for stealing the part she'd wanted. She even accused me of talking behind her back, of plotting to get that part just because I knew she had wanted it. I tried to explain that I hadn't even known about the part, much less known that she'd wanted it, but she wouldn't listen. She kept on ranting and raving and cursing me. Then she reached out and grabbed me by the hair, telling me that she wasn't going to let me plot against her anymore. I struggled to get away but she was a much larger woman than I and far, far angrier. I think her anger must have given her extra strength. She shoved me toward the railing, telling me that she was going to do what she should have done years ago: she was going to kill me."

Carla stopped, closed her eyes momentarily, and shuddered. Then she opened them once again and stared out blankly. "I didn't really believe she was serious about killing me until she had half of my body jackknifed over the railing. I clutched at the rail and screamed for her to stop, but she kept on pushing, harder and harder. I remember seeing the marble floor far beneath me. It seemed like a very long way down. And I didn't want to die. What had I done to deserve such a horrible end?

"Then I got lucky. The Persian rug under my mother's feet slipped and she lost her hold on me. I managed to scramble back onto solid ground, but just as I thought I was safe, she lunged for me. I sidestepped her and tried to push her away. I remember thinking that it was she who ought to go over that railing, not me. She deserved it for making my life such hell. And then I got my wish. I moved away as she went for me again. She was pushing so hard that when she hit the railing, her body flipped over the top. She grabbed at me, and yelled at me to save her, but it happened so fast that I couldn't have, even if I'd wanted to." Covering her face with her hands, Carla began to sob. "I'll never forget her screams or the sound of her body hitting the floor."

"Carla, my love," Drake whispered, taking her into his arms. He wanted to erase it all—the pain, the loneliness, the memories. He wanted to make her whole again. He caressed her, showing with gently stroking fingers how much he cared for her. "You didn't murder your mother; it was an accident. My God, she was trying to kill you. She deserved something far worse than what happened."

"Afterward, I ran downstairs," Carla broke in, needing to finish her story—it had been bottled up inside her for so long. "I thought she might still be alive. She wasn't." She buried her face against his chest and wept. "It was just awful."

"So what happened next?" Drake asked, holding her tightly as he stroked her hair, her neck and her back.

"It's all kind of blurry," Carla admitted in a muffled voice. "I was in shock, of course. I remember thinking that I should call the police. But I just couldn't face them—not alone, not yet. So I called my mother's psychiatrist, Dr. Cook, instead. He had always been kind to me. I vaguely remember him taking me into the living room and asking me what had happened. After I had told him, he ordered me to bed with a strong dose of sleeping pills. I was already asleep when the police arrived.

"It was two days before mother's psychiatrist would let the police see me. I was so drugged and confused at the time that at first I believed the story he told me when I woke up. He said that my mother had slipped on the carpet going up to bed; that I had heard her scream and when I came out to investigate, she was already dead. The doctor lied to protect me. He had often wondered whether my mother beat me; he knew of her temper and violent nature better than anyone. But it was only a suspicion on his part; Mother was too clever to admit to anyone that she used to physically abuse me. I suppose lying to the police was Dr. Cook's way of salving his guilty conscience."

Carla brushed away a lock of hair that had fallen over her eye and smiled tremulously. "I suppose he was right to do what he did. I should be grateful. If the press had discovered what had really happened that night, they would never have left me alone. And I certainly wasn't strong enough to take that on top of everything else that had happened." She sighed. "Still, it left me feeling very confused for many years. I used to have nightmares about that night. I'd dream that Mother was trying to push me over that railing. Just when I was about to go over, I'd wake up screaming. None of it made sense. Finally, years later, I tracked the doctor down and confronted him with the story of my nightmares. It was then that he told me what had really occurred."

"It's okay, honey," Drake said, leaning down and kissing away the tears streaking her face. "It's all over. It's all passed." Pulling her down on the bed, he began to stroke her. Gradually, he felt the tension begin to seep from her body as she became calm.

"You can see why I've shied away from reporters and the public," she explained, relaxing under the feel of his hands touching her body. For the first time in years, she felt peaceful and free. Free to love, free to be happy. Drake knew the worst about her and he hadn't rejected her; he still loved her. She went on, "What would happen if I were to accidentally slip and tell the truth? I wouldn't ruin just my life; I'd ruin Dr. Cook's life too. He lied to protect me. If the police found out what he'd done, they could take away his medical license."

"I wouldn't worry about it," Drake said, touching her cheek and smiling gently. "You didn't ask him to lie; he did that on his own. And anyway, you have nothing to hide. Your conscience should be clear. Your mother tried to kill you. What happened to her was an accident.''

''I know that intellectually,'' she murmured. ''But I still feel the guilt. Maybe I always will. If I had been more understanding... If I'd stayed locked in my room...''

''There's one thing I learned long ago,'' Drake said, pulling her down on the bed and protectively covering her body with his. ''You can't rewrite the past. You can learn from it, you can make the future better because of it, but you can't change it.'' He rubbed his face against hers. ''So stop worrying about it. What happened long ago formed you. It wasn't pleasant, but it made you what you are.'' Looking at her sternly, he added, ''And it wasn't your fault. Do you hear me?'' He raised his head and looked deep into her eyes. Carla saw compassion and love shining in their amber depths. He murmured, ''I said, do you hear me? It wasn't your fault. Now repeat after me: It wasn't my fault.''

''It wasn't my fault,'' she replied huskily. ''And thanks for listening to me. I feel better already.''

''Now that I know everything there is to know about you, will you marry me? My offer still goes.''

''Oh, Drake. Why do you have to be so sweet and so persistent?'' Carla asked. She knew that if he kept being such a wonderful man, she would never be able to say no to anything he suggested. ''Can't you ease up a little? Give me some more time?''

"For you, lady, anything," he said. Raking a hand through his curly brown hair, he added, "Even the impossible. And I may find looking at you without touching you next to impossible."

"Oh, you can still touch me," Carla assured him as she ran her fingers along the smooth-textured skin of his back. "We'll just have to be discreet."

"They say that discretion is the better part of valor," Drake said, leaning over and nibbling at her ear. The heat of his breath against Carla's sensitive skin was a potent aphrodisiac.

"If we were valorous, we'd go do those dishes that have been waiting for us all morning," Carla said, as her hands fumbled for the clasp of his shorts. With shaky hands, she unfastened them.

"Who wants to be valorous?" Drake asked, as his hands slipped under her T-shirt. "Certainly not me."

"Me neither," Carla agreed, sliding down the zipper of his shorts. Then her hands slipped under the elastic of his briefs. She felt the stretch of cotton fabric on the back of her hands. Spreading her fingers, she kneaded his buttocks as she pressed his body into her.

"Witch," Drake said, letting out a guttural moan.

It was waiting for them once again—the hunger, the need, the desperate urge to be one. Her hands were eager and seeking as they stripped the cutoffs away from his body. His hands were equally fevered and intense as he slid the T-shirt over her head.

Warm sunlight glanced through the window and splayed across their bodies. Outside a bird sang in a nearby tree. A motorboat stuttered by, upsetting the smooth, glassy surface of the lake. But they were oblivious to it all. They only knew each other. They only needed each other. Nothing else. Nothing more.

The next morning shone bright with promise, but Carla awoke feeling as though she were about to be tried. She'd either prove herself or make a fool of herself. It was the day of her first practice session with Drake's brothers.

Even the giddy euphoria of being in love and being loved couldn't dispel her anxiety. She'd greedily wolfed down breakfast like a lumberjack, then realized after she'd finished that she hadn't eaten breakfast because she was hungry; she'd eaten breakfast because she was nervous.

"You're awfully quiet this morning," Drake remarked, as he accompanied Carla to the sound studio. "What's wrong? Are you nervous?"

"Yes, a little," Carla confessed, directing her eyes toward the rock-strewn path.

Drake leaned over and draped an arm around Carla, giving her a squeeze. "Don't worry. You're gonna be great."

"Do you really think so?" Carla asked, shooting him a hesitant glance. Normally she hated fishing for compliments, but at the moment she needed all the confidence she could beg, borrow or steal.

"I know so." Stopping, he turned her toward him and raised her chin so that he could look deep into her eyes. "You keep forgetting, I know you better than you know yourself. I know all your secrets and—'' he smiled, flashing straight, gleaming white teeth at her ''—and all your vulnerabilities. Also your strengths. And I love you the better because of them." Reading the doubt in Carla's eyes, he added, "Ah, I see you don't believe me. Good. I'd be glad to give you a reminder."

He leaned down and kissed her. Doubt and uncertainty took wing and flew away. So did reason—momentarily. It took the sound of voices calling to one another to awaken Carla from her passionate reverie. She said a trifle breathlessly, "I don't think this is what I'd call being discreet. Don't you think we'd better get going?"

Drake grinned ruefully. "I knew this was going to drive me bonkers. Come on, let's go."

The cabin housing the recording studio was situated not far from the main house. Carla clattered up the wooden steps, then entered through the door, her eyes sweeping the place in a single glance. It was a large rectangular room furnished with dilapidated rattan furniture. Beige carpeting covered the floors and walls. On the walls were personally autographed posters from other well-known rock bands. Carla noted that it was a typical Lanning-style room—unpretentious, but comfortable. But the musical paraphernalia was another matter. Drake's band wasn't just a bunch of guys who got together and sang and played guitar; drums, saxophone, trumpet, trombone, even clarinet, were included in the group's musical repertoire.

The other band members were already in place and practicing when Drake and Carla arrived. Carla sat down on the couch and waited to be called. And she waited. And she waited some more.

Time limped by and Carla began to get impatient. What was it with these guys, she thought grumpily, crossing one blue-jeaned leg over the other. Why had Drake gone to all the trouble of getting her here if he wasn't going to let her perform? She'd been sitting on the couch for hours, and so far no one had even asked her if she could tell a quarter note from a half note.

She couldn't help feeling bored. They'd practiced one song over and over again and still Drake wasn't satisfied. If Drake had asked her opinion, she could have told him what was wrong. The beat needed to be slowed down. The song was supposed to be a sexy, sultry love song, but at the speed they were doing it, it sounded ridiculous—like a 33-RPM record being played at 78 RPM.

When they started the song over once again, Carla could take no more. Jumping up from the couch, she said, "I've heard the Monday-morning garbage pickup make better music than that."

Signaling for the band to stop, Drake turned and grinned. Bowing, he said, "Okay, lady. If you're so smart, tell me what we're doing wrong."

"I thought you'd never ask," Carla replied with a sweet smile. The smile was a desperate attempt to hide the tremors suddenly quaking through her body.

"I'll play it on the piano and you can tell me what you think," she suggested, sitting down on the piano bench.

Her hands were shaking as they flipped to the first page of the sheet music. She was positive that her fingers were so cold and clammy that she would never be able to control their motion on the keyboard. For a long moment, she stared at the keyboard in sheer panic.

"You can do it. We know you can show us up," Drake murmured softly.

She lifted her eyes at the sound of his voice. She'd been so lost in thought that she hadn't realized that Drake had walked over to the piano. Standing just a few feet away, he was looking at her with eyes so compelling they would make a hypnotist seem wishy-washy.

"You're right." She paused and then nodded. "You're absolutely right."

Her eyes shifted to the keyboard. Steady, girl, she told herself. You know you can do it. Lifting her arms, she stretched her hands over the black and white keys. For a moment they hovered, and then Carla plunged, like a swimmer diving into cold water. Miraculously, the water felt fine. The moment she heard the trickle of keys her nervousness washed away. Music was fluid and so was she.

She was transported to another time, another place. A time in her life when she was still young and full of ideals. Music did that for her. It always had. She supposed it always would.

There was a wide round of applause when Carla finished the song. Drake stepped around the piano, picked Carla up in his arms and whirled her around. Then he stopped, set her back down on her feet, and leaned over and kissed her lightly on the lips. The devilish glint in his eyes told Carla that he'd like to do more. "You're some lady. And you sure can sing." He looked up at his brothers, who had crowded around them, and asked, "What do you think? Would you like to do a concert with Carla Fox?"

"Sure," everyone agreed.

Bobby's voice penetrated the enthusiastic laughter and shouting. He stepped forward. "I thought Drake was nuts when he told me he was going to do a concert with you." He grinned apologetically at Carla as he said this and added, "Don't take offense. I was still thinking of you as Miss Foster. It was hard to imagine you as Carla Fox. But now that I've heard you I take it all back. I can hardly wait for the Hollywood Bowl. We're gonna knock 'em dead!"

"Thank you, Bobby," said Carla, giving him an impulsive hug. "I know you wouldn't say that unless you really meant it."

Afternoon became evening and still they practiced. Like mild-mannered Dr. Jekyll, Drake became another person. He was still dictatorial, but now he was demanding. He was still energetic, but now he was driven.

Around six o'clock they stopped briefly to raid the refrigerator in the kitchenette. After gulping down ham sandwiches and beer, they were once again back at work.

A few hours later, Carla readjusted the headphones on her ears. Her head was aching. Her eyes felt as if someone were trying an exotic form of torture by pulling the eyeballs out of their sockets. But still they practiced. And Carla felt progressively worse and worse.

She knew that she ought to confess to everyone that she was too tired to perform anymore, but no, she was too proud and too stubborn. She wasn't about to be the one to call it quits. If they could take it, so could she.

They had just started another song when Carla's voice began to falter. The band stopped momentarily and stared at her. Carla felt her face begin to flush. She apologized. "Sorry, let's take it from the top again."

Drake, who was standing nearby, took a careful look at her and motioned for the band to go. "Okay, class dismissed. I'll see you guys tomorrow at the crack of noon."

As everyone shuffled out of the room, Carla was aware of the steady, firm grip of Drake's hand as he led her toward the couch. She settled onto the cushions and closed her eyes. Colors and swirling shapes swam on the darkened lids of her eyes.

"Here, take this."

As her eyelids fluttered open, she felt a stab of pain shoot through her head. She winced as she looked at the two white tablets he held out.

"It's aspirin. Here's some water."

She accepted the pills and swallowed them with a gulp. "Thanks."

"The next time you start to feel bad, I want you to tell me right away. There's no sense in being a martyr," Drake instructed her, sitting down. "Here, lie down on the couch and put your head on my lap. I'll give you a head massage."

"Mmm, that feels good," said Carla as she felt his fingers begin to probe and knead the pain away from her temple. She closed her eyes and sighed in relief.

"Why didn't you tell me you had a headache?"

Her eyelids fluttered open briefly and then closed. "I didn't want to interrupt our practice session."

His voice was rough with disapproval. "I know I can be a bit pushy at times, but I'm not a slave driver. Please tell me when you get tired. After all, Simon Legree went out with hoop skirts."

"Imagine you knowing who Simon Legree was," Carla said dreamily, liking the feel of his knowing fingers against her skull.

"*Uncle Tom's Cabin* was required reading for tenth grade," he said, as he massaged the base of her head with deft fingers. "I ought to know. I did my book report from the *Cliffs Notes*."

"Shame on you," Carla murmured, feeling relaxed and very comfortable. "Just when I was beginning to think you were a real intellectual."

Her eyes flickered open when his fingers stopped. He said, "I think you're ready for bed."

She lifted her arms, reached around to the back of his neck and pulled his mouth to hers. "I think you're right," she whispered as her lips found his.

She felt the flick of his tongue inside her mouth, and his fingers as he touched her breasts. She wanted more, much more—and then some.

Drake lifted his head and regarded her intently. His eyes were almost as dark as the thick eyelashes that framed them. He whispered throatily, "I thought we were going to be discreet."

"I thought we were, too," she said, pulling his head back to hers. She traced the line of his lips with her tongue and added, "But I don't seem to be feeling very discreet at the moment."

He planted a lingering kiss on her mouth, then raised his head and suggested, "The door's unlocked. Anyone could walk in. Shall I go and lock it?"

"Sure," Carla said, reluctantly letting go of him. "I guess I can wait that long. But hurry."

She watched as he rose and started to walk across the room. She liked everything there was about this man: his body, his walk, his sensitivity—especially his sensitivity. With his lithe, animal grace, he reached for the lock on the door. His hand stopped in midair as the door suddenly swung open of its own accord.

A balding, middle-aged man bustled through the door. He had a large, drooping potbelly that made him look almost as wide as he was tall. White polyester pants, a white polo shirt and matching white patent-leather belt and shoes didn't make him look any taller or slimmer, either. Rubbing his hands together gleefully, he exclaimed in a booming voice, "Drake! There you are! I've been wandering all over God's little green earth looking for you."

"Hi, Sid," Drake responded unenthusiastically. Sid Duffy was publicity director for Performance Records, the record company to which he was under contract. He was also a royal pain in the butt. When it came time for Drake to renew his contract, he had no intention of signing with Performance Records again. And Sid was the major reason why.

"Sid Duffy's the name, publicity's the game," Sid said, marching across the room. Bending down, he offered a chubby hand to Carla. "You're Carla Fox. I'd recognize you anywhere."

"Hello, Mr. Duffy," Carla said, sending Drake a questioning glance.

"Sid's publicity director for Performance Records," Drake informed her, walking across the room. He shot Carla a warning look and added, "How did you find me, Sid? I don't remember telling you I'd be here."

"Alan told me where you were," Sid replied, flashing a slick smile that was meant to be ingratiating.

"My compliments go out to you, Sid," Drake said curtly. Silently, he cursed his agent. He should have known Alan wouldn't keep the secret. All you had to do was shove a little money under Alan's nose and he'd follow you anywhere. The hostility in Drake's voice was barely tethered when he said, "You did an excellent job of worming that piece of information out

of Alan, He had explicit instructions not to tell anyone where I was."

"I guess he figured I wasn't just anyone," Sid
boasted, apparently oblivious to the negative vibra-
tions Drake was sending out. He wagged a fat finger
at Drake. "And I must say, I'm annoyed with you.
How do you think I—" he patted his sloping chest a
couple of times "—felt when the news of this concert
was announced?" Drake started to speak, but was cut
off. "Well, I'll tell you how I felt. It's a four-letter
word and you can say it in front of a lady." He bowed
to Carla. "The word is hurt. Capital *h-u-r-t*. Really
hurt. You think up the hottest charity-publicity gimmick in town and you don't even tell me about it! How
do you think that makes me look when the reporters
come to ask questions? I'll tell you how that makes me
look: stupid. And that's a six-letter word that ought to
be a four-letter word!"

"This isn't a publicity gimmick," Drake began,
dragging a hand through his hair and trying to keep
hold of his temper. Motioning by a nod of the head for
Carla to leave the room, he continued, "Now, I'm
sorry if my not telling you about the concert embarrassed you in front of the press. Maybe I should have
warned you. Quite frankly, it never occurred to me.
This concert has nothing to do with you and Performance Records."

"Nothing to do with Performance Records," Sid
echoed. "You seem to be forgetting one very important fact—we have a contract with you."

"You have a contract for my recordings, not for my live performances," Drake corrected him. "Since we won't be recording the concert, you're not involved."

"Oh, no, you don't," Sid said, wagging a finger at Drake. "I'm not going to let every bootleg record company on the face of this earth get one up on me. I'm—" he patted his chest emphatically "—doing the recording. And I've got plans for a video that will knock your socks off."

"No recording. No video." Drake's tone was terse and tight. "And that's final."

Sidney shook his head sadly. "I didn't want to get tough with you, my boy, but it looks like I'm going to have to. You didn't read the fine print in that contract of yours carefully enough. I know you think you're smart, but you aren't smart enough to get around me. You've got the right to do live performances on your own, yes. But it clearly states in the contract that you have to give Performance Records ninety days' written notice. Since you neglected to do that, you're in violation of contract. Go ahead and try to do this concert without my cooperation. I'll have a court order to shut you down before your fans ever get near the ticket office."

Chapter Eleven

Carla rose from the couch quietly. She hated to leave such an interesting conversation, especially one so vital to her own future, but she knew it would do her no good to get involved in this discussion. Drake already knew that she had good reasons for not wanting to do the concert. He must also realize that she could do no more than what she'd already agreed to do. Otherwise it would be impossible to keep her present identity a secret.

She was halfway to the door when Sid stopped her short. "Hey, you! Little lady. Carla! Don't leave now. You're the reason I drove all the way up here. I have a contract that will make you rich."

"I don't want to be rich," Carla mumbled, quickening her steps toward the door.

"You don't want to be rich," Sid repeated, surprising them both by the speed with which he bounded over to the door. Grabbing Carla's arm, he pulled her back. "Ha! That's a good one."

Carla stopped and stared at him, wondering why he couldn't take the hint. Slowly, with all the dignity she could muster, she disengaged her arm from his clasp. Her tone was icy. "Believe me, Mr. Duffy, I don't want to be rich. I've been there before and it wasn't a pleasant trip."

"You were just movin' with the wrong crowd," he assured her. "Anyway, I always say never say no until you've seen the dollars-and-cents signs and the bottom line. That way, you know what you're missing out on. And you'd be missing out on plenty, let me tell you. Yes, ma'am, I've got an offer here that nobody in their right mind would refuse."

"Leave Carla out of this," Drake advised in a barely controlled voice. His long legs ate up the distance as he quickly crossed the room. "If you have any offers—or threats, for that matter—you'd better talk to me first."

"It's okay," Carla replied, surprising both Drake and herself by her calm and contained manner. Laying a restraining hand on Drake's arm, she added, "I appreciate your enthusiasm, Mr. Duffy, but really, I'm not interested."

Sid dismissed her words with a wide flourish of his hand. "I know that line. I've used it myself, time and time again. It just means you want to play hardball. In other words, big bucks. But don't you worry your pretty little head. We're talking major leagues here. The quarterback has already given me the handoff to go as high as fifty thousand smackeroos."

"You're mixing your metaphors, and anyway, that's a damned paltry offer," Drake broke in. He pulled Sid aside and, pointing toward the door, motioned for Carla to leave. "She's already said no. And she's not playing hard to get. She's just not interested."

"You drive a hard bargain," Sid replied, trying to wrench himself from Drake's grasp. He was no match for Drake's size and strength. "But I'm a nice guy. I'll go as high as sixty."

"I've already told you: I'm not interested," Carla said.

"Okay, okay," Sid grumbled as Carla opened the door. "I'll make it seventy-five. But not a penny more!"

"I don't care if it's a million. I'm still not interested." Carla slammed the door shut with a bang.

Having trouble getting to sleep was becoming the rule not the exception for Carla. She tossed in her bed, wishing she had the nerve to walk down to Drake's cabin. She missed him. She wanted him. She needed him.

More than that, she was curious to know the outcome of Drake's conversation with Sidney.

Could Sid really close down the concert? He'd seemed very sure of himself. But men such as Sid were often mostly bluff and bluster. And closing down the concert would bring a lot of bad publicity to Performance Records. Would they risk it? Was that possible?

She heard a soft rapping and then the door squeaked slowly open. A muffled voice whispered, "Carla? Are you still awake?"

"Yes, of course," Carla answered, sitting up. "Drake, what happened?"

The moonlight was not nearly as brilliant as it had been several nights ago, but still she could see him stalking across her room. She felt the mattress heave and sigh as he settled himself down on the bed close to her. He caught her long slender fingers in his hands and raising them to his mouth, kissed each and every digit. He remarked nonchalantly, "I've called off the concert."

"You've called off the concert!" Carla cried in dismay. Her fingers gripped his hand tightly as she protested, "But you can't do that!"

He sighed heavily. "It seems there's no other way. I called my attorney and found out Sid was absolutely right—he could shut us down." Drake kissed her fingers once again, then let his lips travel hungrily up her arm. "Don't worry. The kids will still get their money. It'll just have to come out of my own pocket instead."

"You can't do that!" Carla protested, snatching away her arm. "Why, you promised us half a million dollars."

He let out a low, throaty laugh. In the dim light, she could see the gleam of white teeth as he smiled. "So you still don't trust me, huh? Don't worry. I'm good for it."

"But that's not the point," Carla said, twisting around in her bed and plumping the pillows up. She lay back, then said, "It's not a matter of the money at all. It's a matter of my promising to do something—of not going back on my word. I've always always hated doing that. Even the thought of it raises the prickles on my back. There are going to be a lot of disappointed people if we pull out now."

"I know." He sighed and raised an arm to sweep the hair from his face. "But don't forget, I also made a promise to you: absolutely no publicity; just this one concert. Now something's happened and I'm unable to keep that promise. And keeping my promise to you means more to me. You're the most important thing in my life. I can do without the concert. I can't do without you. So the answer's simple. We have to cancel the concert."

"But I don't want to cancel the concert," she objected. Her fists pounded the mattress emphatically. "Damn it, I was looking forward to it. I want to do it."

"Even if it means doing a video, too," Drake asked, shooting her a searching glance. "I'm sorry, but my hands are tied. If I go ahead with the concert, I have to let Performance Records do the video."

Carla took a deep breath. Talk about burning your bridges. She was about to set a keg of dynamite under hers. Letting her breath out with a long sigh, she said, "Even if it means doing the video, too."

"I can't promise you anonymity anymore," Drake pointed out. "There'll be people working on the video I don't know all that well. I can promise to try to keep things secret, but it may not work."

She closed her eyes and let her mind empty momentarily. Then she opened her eyes once again. "I understand that, but I still want to do it."

He leaned over and gave her a big hug. "That's my girl. I was hoping you'd say that."

She pushed him away and regarded him suspiciously. The moonlight fell across his face, outlining the rugged, sharply chiseled features of his face. His mouth was twisted in a mischievous smile. "Was all of this just a ruse?" she demanded. "A clever ploy of yours to get your own way? Were you really going to cancel the concert at all?"

He grinned back at her. "Of course I was. But I couldn't help hoping you'd feel the same sense of obligation as me. I was also hoping that you were beginning to enjoy performing with me."

"Speaking of performances..." Carla said, pulling him to her. Her mouth locked onto his for a long, seductive kiss. "How'd you like to practice an impromptu duo right now?"

"That sounds like a good idea to me," was his response.

Carla mistrusted happiness. To her, it had always been a transitory, undependable thing. Happiness beguiled you, made you feel that life could really be a wonderful thing. Then suddenly unhappiness reared its nasty head. It slapped you back down to the ground and made you feel trampled lower than you'd ever felt before.

Carla felt that way about her life now. She was happy, but she didn't quite trust it. In the days and weeks she was with Drake, she could relax and forget about everything but the joy of being with him. But nighttime, when she was alone in her bed, was different.

Drake, who seemed to understand Carla's feelings before she consciously realized they were there, noticed the faint tension around her eyes. It didn't take him long to figure out what was wrong. She needed more time, he decided. A lifetime, really. But as practice session after practice session elapsed, the minutes and hours until the concert became fewer. And Carla became more and more nervous. Drake knew he was running out of time fast.

Whenever he mentioned the idea of getting married—before the concert, after it, or at anytime—she looked wary and doubtful and promptly changed the subject. And she still hadn't told him she loved him.

Those were just words, he reassured himself. Even if she didn't say it, he knew she loved him. He could tell from the gentle look in her eyes when she watched him. He could tell from the way she touched him.

He knew she was running scared because of her unhappy childhood. She was afraid of getting too closely involved. He had no intention of letting her past ruin her future... or their life together. He decided to do something drastic.

Drake waited for the right moment to approach her. The right moment came on a Monday evening, exactly one week away from the date of the concert. The family had all gone into town to see the latest Sylvester Stallone movie while Carla and Drake had decided to stay at home and do some extra "practicing." The practicing had ended up in bed, of course.

A glowing red sunset basked warm light across their tired, but pleasantly replete bodies. They lay upon the bed in Drake's room. Drake pulled himself up on one elbow and tenderly stroked the rounded curve of her neck and then her arm.

"I have to leave tomorrow for a few days," he said regretfully, trailing his fingers across her breasts.

She was drowsy, almost asleep, but his words pulled her out of her dreamworld. She opened her eyes and said, "What? You're leaving? Why? Where are you going?"

"Back to L.A. I got a call from Sid this morning. He needs me to help figure out where they're going to put the video cameras during the performance. If I don't go, you can bet that he'll mess it up." He made a face. "I also need to dissuade him from his latest brainstorm. He was talking about hiring the Raiders' cheerleaders to dance for us in the video."

Carla regarded him disbelievingly. "You're kidding!"

He laughed. "Would I kid about such a terrible idea?"

"I hope not." She shook her head. "I gather you told him no to the Raiders' cheerleaders?"

He leaned over and lightly brushed his lips against hers. "What do you think, my love?"

She wrapped her arms around his neck and said huskily, "I don't know what to think when you're near me like this."

He looked at her searchingly, then asked after a short pause, "Want to come along? Bobby's going to stay here. That big house of mine is going to seem mighty lonely without you there."

"I wouldn't want you to be lonely," Carla said, pulling his mouth down to hers. "Who knows what trouble you might get into? Yes, of course I'll come with you."

Pretending to be a married woman could become habit forming, Carla mused as she bent her head over the stove and stirred a large pot simmering with beef and onions. Whoever would have thought that cooking could be so satisfying to the soul? She withdrew the spoon, blew on it, then tasted. Delicious, she thought. Belgian beer stew. If Drake didn't like it, it would just leave more for her to eat.

She'd never played the role of housewife before and she was enjoying it to the hilt. Perhaps Drake was right; maybe they should get married. Somehow they would manage to clear all the obstacles out of their way. Certainly the thought of going back to her old life—alone—was unappealing.

She lifted the top of another pot, where water was frothing and beginning to boil, and switched the gas to off. When Drake got home, it would take just a few minutes to heat up the water to cook the noodles.

She heard the tinkle of dog tags clattering against one another. It was Lady Catherine de Bourgh, Carla's wire-haired terrier. Drake had pitched a fit when he'd discovered that Carla had a dog she'd left behind with Elizabeth. "Families stick together," he'd reminded her. "From now on, Lady Catherine goes where we go."

Carla dipped her spoon into the pot again, found a large chunk of meat, then set it down on the spoon rest to cool. She glanced at the clock. It was time to uncork the bottle of burgundy to let it breathe. Drake would be home soon.

She opened the wine, then fed Lady Catherine her treat of cooled meat. Next she made her way toward the dining room, checking to make sure that the china set on a yellow linen tablecloth was all in order. It was, as were the shimmering crystal wineglasses and the bird-of-paradise flower arrangement she'd made earlier that day.

With nothing left to do, she wandered to the living room to make sure that everything was in order. Dolores, Drake's maid, had been given a week's paid vacation, so Carla had taken it upon herself to keep the place tidy. She enjoyed doing something for Drake, even something so small.

Everything was in place, just as she'd expected. She couldn't help grinning as her eyes scanned the room.

Her house never looked this neat. What was Drake going to think when he discovered she was actually the world's worst housekeeper? She'd warned him often enough, and he'd seen her house that one time, but still ... And if they had children, the mess would multiply at an exponential rate.

Children. That idea stopped her short. It made her smile and feel happy all over. How wonderful it would be to bear Drake's children. He'd make a wonderful father. She couldn't ask for more from her life.

Tonight was the night, she suddenly decided. If Drake asked her to marry him tonight, she'd say yes. It was a gamble, but if Drake was willing to risk it, so was she.

A piece of sheet music lying on the piano caught her attention. It was a song she'd been working on secretly for days. She'd composed it herself and intended to sing it for Drake as a surprise. It put into song all the feelings and love she found so hard to express in words.

She thought the song was good—she was almost positive it was good. But she'd never composed a song before and she was uncertain how Drake would react.

When Drake entered through the front door several minutes later, the sound of music greeted his ears. His steps quickened toward the living room until he reached the threshold, where he stood still, transfixed.

Carla sat at the piano, her hair billowing over her shoulders like a cloud of yellow-spun cotton candy. Wearing turquoise Chinese silk lounging pajamas that caressed the soft curves of her body, she looked slender, confident and proudly sensual.

She looked up, smiled when she saw him, and continued to sing, her eyes steady on him, her hands flitting across the keyboard. From the expression on her face, he knew that the song was meant for him. He strained his ears to catch the words. It was a song about love, but the words were unfamiliar.

There was something different about her tonight, he noted. As he listened, he tried to decide what it was. Her smile was freer and less inhibited, her eyes lacked that worried look. She looked happy, sure of herself—as if she'd finally made peace with herself.

He could barely contain himself until she finished. He knew that later he would want to hear that song over and over again, but now a question was burning in his soul.

He made himself count to ten when her hands slowly stilled over the keyboard. It was the longest ten seconds of his life. His voice never wavered, but his heart skipped a beat when he said, "This is the last time I'm going to bring this subject up. I love you. I want to be with you forever. Will you marry me?"

"Of course," she responded, rising from the piano bench and running to him. "I love you, too. I thought you'd never ask."

"I've asked too damn often," Drake replied roughly. He took her in his arms and captured her lips in a smoldering, violent kiss.

* * *

They had made love and talked until the early hours of the morning, so it was no great surprise that they overslept. When the alarm clock finally rang, they discovered that Drake had mistakenly set the alarm for the time he was supposed to be at his appointment, not the hour before.

"Go take your shower and get dressed," Carla instructed him, picking up a diaphanous peach-colored nightgown. Throwing the flimsy material over her head, she added, "I'll go make the coffee. You'll have to drink it on the road, but at least you'll have some caffeine in your system."

"I knew I was right to fall in love with you," Drake said cheerfully as he swaggered nude toward the shower. Carla caught a retreating glimpse of his shapely, firm buttocks before she turned and headed for the kitchen.

Soon the teakettle was singing and Carla was dumping hot water into the top of the coffee maker. The coffee had just finished dripping when Drake walked into the room.

"I'll try and be back as soon as possible," he said, tucking a blue T-shirt that read The San Andreas Is My Fault into his blue jeans. Wrapping his arms around Carla he gave her a playful bite on the neck, then went on, "We've got an important date with the jeweler today. What do you fancy for an engagement ring? Diamonds? Sapphires? Or emeralds? Or maybe all three?"

Carla made a face. "That sounds awfully gaudy. Why don't we just settle for a plain band of gold?"

He laughed and dropped a kiss on her cheek. "I bet you're the only woman in town who thinks diamonds are gaudy. But maybe you'll change your mind at the jeweler's. And we'll be ordering two gold bands. One for you and one for me. I have no intention of letting anyone forget that I'm married to you." He leaned over and gave her a long, deep kiss.

"You're never going to make that appointment if you don't leave now," Carla said, coming up for air a few minutes later. Pushing him gently away, she turned and filled a mug with coffee.

Drake took the mug from her hands and tasted it "Delicious. But not nearly as delicious as you." Then he leaned over, gave her a quick kiss and marched toward the door.

When Drake had gone, Carla poured a cup of coffee for herself and went into the living room. Sitting down on the couch, she thought about the past evening, trying to recapture all the words, smiles and actions that told her that Drake loved her.

She was still lost in thought when she noticed Lady Catherine, who'd been sitting on the couch next to her, prick up her ears and bound for the hallway. Carla followed her toward the front door, where she heard someone struggling to open the front door with a key.

Thinking Drake must have forgotten something, Carla quickened her steps. As the door started to swing open, she called, "That's what you get for keeping me up all last night. Now you're really going to be late for that appoint—" She stopped abruptly when she realized that it wasn't Drake opening the door. It was a woman—a shapely-looking brunette, to be precise. She was wearing high heels, white short shorts, and a white tube top that barely covered her.

The woman looked at Carla and demanded, "Who are you? What are you doing here?"

"I could ask the same thing of you," Carla replied coldly. She'd recognized her as Angie, but Carla wasn't about to admit it to her.

"I'm Angie, Drake's girlfriend. I've been out of town for a few weeks," Angie said belligerently, taking a step toward her. She regarded Carla from head to toe, taking in Carla's flimsy nightgown and the unkempt state of her hair. She added contemptuously, "It looks like Drake must have gotten lonely and called for a temporary."

"I'm no temporary," Carla said, trying to keep hold of her temper.

"You look familiar," Angie said. She planted her hands on her hips and cocked her head to the side. The light of understanding suddenly dawned on her face and she smiled slowly. "Now I know who you are. You're the social worker—what's your name? I should be able to remember it—Drake was so angry at you."

"I think you'd better go," Carla advised her. "I don't know how you got a key to Drake's home but I'm sure he wouldn't appreciate your walking in uninvited."

"Oh, Drake won't mind. I'm sure he'll be glad I'm back in town." Angie looked Carla over. "Now you—you're another story. Do you think Drake's going to want you here when he finds out I'm back in town? And what about that high-and-mighty orphanage you work for? What would they say if they knew what was going on?''

"That's none of your business," replied Carla stiffly. "Now, I really think you should leave."

"I don't feel like leaving," Angie said. She strutted toward the living room, her high heels making a clattering sound as they hit the tiled floor. "But you can leave if you don't like me here. Feel free."

Carla bit her lip. Although Drake had promised to return soon, she had no idea who he was visiting or where he had gone. She was sure he'd straighten this whole thing out. He'd promised that Angie was history. But she couldn't leave Angie alone in Drake's house, even if she knew where to find him. She followed Angie to the living room.

"I must say I was surprised even to find Drake at home," Angie said, sinking down on a couch. "All you read about in the papers lately is Drake and Carla Fox's upcoming concert. I figured for sure they'd be holed away someplace practicing."

Carla smiled politely but didn't speak. What was there for her to say?

Angie didn't seem to notice or care about Carla's disinterest. "Now this Fox dame has got me curious. I could get jealous of her easily. She's got some reputation." She glanced up and noticed Carla's bored look. She played with a ring on her finger and looked as though she were looking for something to say— something to get under Carla's skin. She smiled suddenly. "See this? Drake gave it to me a couple of months ago. Nice, huh? Diamonds." She looked at Carla and asked, "What did he give you?"

Carla turned and walked toward the French windows, then stood and stared for a long moment. Drake had suggested giving her diamonds also. Was that just his normal patter? Were there dozens of women walking around wearing Drake Lanning diamonds?

"There's something about you that's bugging me," Angie said, interrupting Carla's thoughts.

Carla kept her face averted toward the window. With a sinking feeling in her gut, she knew that she was about to be exposed, but she felt too numb and upset to fight or even care.

When Carla refused to turn around, Angie stood up and walked across the room. Carla heard the sound of her high heels, then felt the touch of Angie's hand on her shoulder. Carla turned around and regarded her inquiringly. "Yes?"

"Of course. How could I be so stupid?" Angie said, snapping her fingers as comprehension dawned in her eyes. "I know why you look so familiar—you're her. You're Carla Fox!"

Carla moistened her lips and said in a shaking voice, "That's absurd. I'm not Carla Fox. My name's Foster."

"Oh, yes, you are!" Angie cried triumphantly. "You're Carla Fox. Why, imagine hiding away all these years as a social worker. Think what the press would do with such a story!"

"You mustn't say anything," Carla said desperately, deciding that her only chance would be to play on Angie's "affection" for Drake. "Drake would be furious! It would ruin his concert if people were to discover what I'd been doing these past years."

"Why would it ruin it? Was that part of his deal with you? Do you plan to go back to that life after the concert?"

"Well, I had," Carla admitted slowly. "But now, well, I'm not sure."

"Because of Drake, right? You're thinking of marrying him, aren't you?"

Carla said nothing, but Angie seemed to take this as an assent. Letting out an expletive, Angie pivoted on her heels and stalked toward the middle of the room. "All this time I've wasted with him, hoping something would come out of it." She turned and faced Carla, her green eyes bitter, her mouth a thin hard line. "Do you know what I do for a living? I'm an airline hostess. That's a classy word for a flying waitress. I fetch and carry and say 'Yes, sir' to the biggest bunch of bums this side of Pershing Square. I'm not getting any younger and I want out. I figured Drake Lanning was my ticket. And he might have been, if you hadn't come along."

"Look, I'm sorry," Carla began. "I know how it feels to be on your own and alone. Believe me—"

"You don't know how it feels to be alone at all," Angie spat out. "I grew up on the south side of L.A. You grew up in Beverly Hills. You were a star before you even knew how to brush your teeth. Well, let me tell you, I'm tired of losing out to people like you. I'm tired of losing, period. This time I'm going to win. I'm visiting a friend of mine as soon as I leave this house. He's a journalist. He'll know what to do with this story. And I figure he'll pay me plenty for a story like this."

"Please don't do it!" Carla called to Angie's retreating back. "Don't do it! I've got money, too. I'll pay you . . ."

Carla was speaking to thin air. Angie was gone. As the front door slammed, Carla made a quick decision. Heading for the telephone, she dialed a number and requested that a taxi pick her up as soon as possible.

There was no sign of Carla, her belongings, or Lady Catherine when Drake arrived home a half an hour later.

Chapter Twelve

Got nowhere to run. Got nowhere to hide.'' The words to the sixties song were ringing in Carla's ear. Carla paid the taxi driver, thanked him, tucked Lady Catherine under her right arm and carried her suitcase in her left hand. Then she headed for the front door to her house.

She had to get out of this town. She had to be alone to think. But where could she go? Once Angie told Carla's story to the press, her home would no longer be a safe or private haven. Besides, when Drake discovered her missing, her house would be the first place he'd come looking for her.

And she couldn't talk to him—not yet. Not until she'd had a chance to think. In the confused state of mind she was in now, she knew she'd say something she'd later regret.

Adrenaline was pumping blood to her brain in quick spurts. Her heart was hammering, her hands shaking. As she fumbled to pick the keys out of her purse, her trembling fingers let them slip out of her grasp and fall with a clatter against the concrete step. Bending over, Carla retrieved her keys, telling herself to calm down. It took several attempts, but finally she succeeded in opening the door.

The house was as hot and dry and stifling as Death Valley. Setting Lady Catherine down on the floor, she hurried to the bedroom. Lady Catherine followed, sniffing the familiar smells of the house as she went, the metal tags on her collar jingling noisily.

Heading for a tall oak dresser in a corner of the room, Carla pulled open the highest drawer. She saw scarves and a plastic egg from an old pair of panty hose. Letting out a muffled oath for her disorderliness, Carla tried the next drawer. Underwear. She tried the next. No luck again. And the next after that.

Wouldn't you know it would be in the bottom drawer, Carla thought as she pulled out a curly, black-haired wig. She had worn it for Halloween at the orphanage a few years back. Pulling it on her head, she turned to examine herself in the full-length mirror attached to the back of a closet door. She decided that she would never make a convincing brunette with her present pale coloring. Turning around, she bent down and yanked the bottom drawer of her dresser open once again. Her old makeup kit. She opened the plastic cover and began to brush bold dashes of color over her face. It was amazing what makeup could do to change her appearance. After lengthening and darkening her eyebrows with a pencil, she was hardly recognizable—even to herself.

Her clothing wasn't right, however. The shorts she was wearing were much too abbreviated and daring for the old-fashioned hairdo. She stood for a moment, thinking, massaging the back of her neck at the same time. Then she remembered a paper sack filled with old clothing she'd been meaning to give to the Goodwill for years. Opening the closet door, she began to rummage along the floor.

At last she found the brown bag stuffed with clothing from her long-ago college days. When she pulled out the blue and white seersucker culottes with the matching sleeveless shirt, she couldn't help smiling: they were decidedly out of fashion and just what she needed.

Carla's heart was racing as she hurried toward the garage. Lady Catherine, always happy at the prospect of a drive in the car, was wagging her tail happily. Carla opened the car door, let Lady Catherine jump in, then climbed in herself.

Carla had a few scary moments when her Honda, which hadn't been driven in a month, refused to start. But a few well-chosen cusswords convinced the engine to fire and roar to life. She heaved a sigh of relief as the car rolled out of the driveway.

What next? Carla wondered, guiding her car toward the entrance to the Pasadena Freeway. Where do

I go? She'd always heard that the best place to lose yourself was in a big city. But where could she hole up in Los Angeles for a few days without being found? She considered appealing to Elizabeth for help, but she knew Elizabeth was the first person Drake and the press would consult. And Elizabeth didn't always agree with Carla's ideas on keeping her identity secret. Elizabeth would never reveal her whereabouts to the press, but with Drake it would be another story; Elizabeth had already demonstrated she had a real weakness for Drake. No, she couldn't ask Elizabeth.

She needed a town with lots of motels and lots of transients—a place where so many people came and went that no one would be able to trace her.

Anaheim. The home of Disneyland, the California Angels and the dome-shaped Anaheim Convention Center. Knott's Berry Farm was in nearby Buena Park. Anaheim saw more tourists in a day than most towns saw in a year. There were miles upon miles of hotels and motels. No one would ever think to look for her there. And if they did, it would take them days to track her down.

She turned onto the Pasadena Freeway, switched on the radio and pushed the button to her favorite rock station. This was fine while the music lasted, but when the D.J. came on and began to talk about the upcoming Drake Lanning and Carla Fox concert, she switched the radio off in disgust. She needed no reminders that the concert was only two nights away. All that did was bring the nagging question back to mind: What was she going to do?

She tried to shove that unhappy thought aside, though it was easier said than done. She knew that the only way to forget about a problem was to solve it. She would feel no peace until she had decided what to do.

It wasn't long before Carla was taking the exit for Anaheim, a sprawling, typical Los-Angeles-style town with modern stucco buildings and gray asphalt highways. As she wheeled onto Harbor Boulevard, she felt her eyes barraged with brightly colored billboards and lighted neon signs.

A giant sign advertising the Sleepy Hollow Motel caught her eye. Despite her mood, she couldn't help laughing at the ridiculous picture of a nightshirt-clad, stocking-capped mouse galloping along a gloomy roadway lined with Casper-the-Friendly-Ghost-style ghosts. When she noticed that the marquee beneath it read Pets Okay, Kitchenettes Available, she decided that this must be the place for her. The sign had made her laugh. That must be a good omen. She signaled and swung into the parking lot.

Drake's nerves were on edge. He had learned long ago that getting upset didn't change matters, but still, he couldn't help wondering why Carla had left so abruptly. She had seemed so contented and peaceful when he had left her. But when he returned two hours later, she was gone, as were all her possessions. Had she planned to disappear before he left her? He doubted it. No one, especially someone he knew as well as Carla, could be that good an actress. So what had happened to change her mind? Or was it just a case of cold feet?

If he'd been a drinking man, he would have gotten drunk. Instead, he decided to wear himself out with exercise. Slipping into running shorts, a T-shirt, and his favorite running shoes, he let his feet pound the Beverly Hills pavement for a good five miles. When he returned home, he was feeling sweaty but still keyed up. So he dove into the pool and swam laps until he could barely move.

By the time he'd stepped out of the pool he was feeling too tired to be keyed up. Deciding that after all the exercise he deserved a beer, he sauntered barefoot and still dripping wet toward the kitchen. He had just taken his first swallow when the phone began to ring.

His stomach went hollow and filled with butterflies. Was it Carla calling to explain why she'd left? He picked up the receiver, responding curtly, "Drake, here."

"Hi, Drake," said an unfamiliar male voice on the line. "This is Chad Dawson."

Drake stiffened, sorely tempted to hang up the telephone without listening to what Chad had to say. He wondered how Chad had gotten his home phone number. Chad was an entertainment journalist for one of the yellower rags in town. Drake knew that Chad was a friend of Angie's, but Angie had promised that she would never reveal Drake's private telephone number to anyone.

"Hello, Chad," said Drake coolly, but politely. "What can I do for you?"

Chad cleared his throat. "Well, Angie stopped by my office this morning. She's pretty mad at you. It seems she came by your house this morning and found a woman there dressed in a very scanty negligee."

"Damn," Drake muttered to himself.

"You know how women are," Chad continued smoothly. "Anyway, she claims that the woman was Carla Fox. She also says that she first met Carla at your house when she was working as a social worker for the Happy Home Orphanage. I'd like a verification of that story if you don't mind."

"I do mind," Drake snapped. "I have no comment about this whole thing. And you'd better not print that story."

"Oh, we're printing it, all right," Chad responded cheerfully. "After all, the public has a right to know the truth. I just wanted to make sure it *was* true. And from the way you've reacted, it must be. Thanks for the scoop."

"But—" Drake heard the buzz of a dial tone in his ear. He looked at the telephone receiver angrily, then slammed it back in its cradle. He considered calling Chad back and pleading with him not to print the story, but he knew it was useless to even try.

Drake pushed back a lock of curly brown hair that had fallen over his face. He clenched his jaw and his full lips thinned to one long, grim line. Well, at least he knew now why Carla had left.

He found that knowing the answer brought little consolation. He had to find her. He picked up his bottle of beer and took a long, frustrated swig.

* * *

Carla decided that the Sleepy Hollow had been misnamed. It should have been named Sleazy Hollow. There were cigarette burns on the blue chenille bedspread and the blond, 1950s-style furniture. The room reeked of stale tobacco and must. Near the door was a sign that informed her that checkout time was ten o'clock, along with a warning that all valuables had been marked and registered with the local police.

Well, at least the room had a view—of sorts. Carla lay on her bed and gazed out the window at Disneyland's Matterhorn. It looked more like a hot fudge sundae with liquid marshmallow dribbled over the top than the famed Swiss mountain.

Carla took a sip of white wine from the plastic cup that the motel had thoughtfully provided and wished she could be more like Lady Catherine. The dog was having a great time investigating the room and sniffing the unfamiliar smells. To Lady Catherine, life was uncomplicated and simple.

If only her life could be the same. But it never had been and probably never would be. The past would always be there to haunt and torment Carla. That was the lesson she'd learned today.

And it was all her fault. What had she been thinking, to agree to marry Drake? She must have been crazy.

Angie had actually done her a favor. After some calm thinking, Carla had realized that Angie had attacked as a defense mechanism. She had reminded Carla of a truth that Carla had been trying very hard to ignore. A life with Drake would inevitably put her under the eye and scrutiny of the press. And that she must avoid at all costs. It wasn't just for herself that she had to do this; it was for Dr. Cook, too.

Dr. Cook. She'd often wondered how he was doing. She received a Christmas card from him every year, but it had been five years since she'd last seen him. She'd sometimes considered visiting him, but the time, mood and opportunity never seemed to present itself. She had also decided that he, like her, would prefer to keep the past buried and forgotten.

She took a sip of her wine and looked at her watch. It was nearly six o'clock—time for the evening news.

The motel might scrimp on furnishings, but they had splurged on the color TV. Carla got up from the bed and strode across the room to turn it on. Returning to her bed, she settled herself comfortably back against the pillows.

She watched a commercial that had toilets comparing notes on their owners and vowed never to buy that product again. Then Hollywood's most popular gossip reporter, Sabrina Saxon, was flashed on the screen.

"All of you people who have been wondering what Carla Fox has been up to these past ten years—wait no more," said the melodically voiced blonde. She raised her thinly plucked eyebrows and smiled a secret smile that was supposed to make every viewer in the television audience feel that this juicy tidbit was intended for him or her only. "The full story is just around the corner on the six o'clock news. Stay tuned to KLAX."

After that enticing lead-in, the station wasn't about to tell Carla's story first. The two anchors dithered around, telling about a grisly shoot-out that day, a recent drug bust and the latest airline strike. Next came deodorant and laxative commercials. Finally, when Carla thought she could endure no more, the cameras switched to Sabrina Saxon once again. "Now, for the story we've all been waiting for. Whatever happened to Carla Fox? The music world was recently rocked—" she fluttered her eyes demurely and added "—no pun intended, by the way, with the news that Carla Fox would be performing with rock star Drake Lanning in the Hollywood Bowl."

Sabrina looked up from the teleprompter. "Although tickets for this concert have been sold out for weeks, there's been a lot of skepticism from the critics here in town about whether Carla Fox can still deliver a good concert. Ten years is a long time to be away from the stage for anyone, and Carla was just a teenager when she disappeared.

"There've also been a lot of rumors about what Carla's been doing. Some people claimed she'd joined a convent. Others said she'd been in a mental institution. No one seemed to know. Then today, KLAX, in an exclusive interview, discovered what really happened to Carla Fox."

The station switched to a film clip where Sabrina, Angie, and another man introduced as Chad Dawson from *Snoop Magazine* were seated in a semicircle. Carla leaned forward, feeling her stomach tighten as she heard them relay the past ten years of her life in vivid detail. Her assumed name, her work at the orphanage, even her college years, were all discussed.

A recent picture of Carla was flashed on the screen. Then the camera switched to Sabrina once more. "We've been trying to locate Carla Fox all day, but she seems to have disappeared once again. Even Drake Lanning denies knowledge of her present whereabouts. It seems we'll have to wait for the concert for the reappearance of Carla Fox. And you can be sure that station KLAX will be there to keep you informed."

Carla rose from the bed, crossed the room and switched off the television. Then she walked over to a tiny refrigerator and opened the door. Pulling out a bottle of white wine, she refilled her plastic cup. She figured she deserved it. And what was worse, she knew she was going to need it. This promised to be a long, lonely and thought-provoking evening.

Carla awoke the next morning with her mouth tasting like the bottom of a bird cage. Groaning, she flipped over on her back and tried to go back to sleep.

"I don't believe I drank the whole thing," she moaned, as she lifted a puffy eyelid and noticed the empty bottle of wine standing on the bureau. Her head felt as though it were stuffed with kapok.

Going back to sleep was useless. Thinking that a couple of aspirins and a hot shower might revive her, she dragged herself out of bed.

The spray from the hot water soon misted the small bathroom. Carla stepped inside the shower, enjoying the feel of the warm water pelting her skin. Long, hot showers were one of her favorite vices. At home they always lasted until the hot water ran out. As she soaped her body, she couldn't help remembering the last time she'd taken a shower. That time, Drake had done the soaping up and rinsing. They'd ended up making love on the tiled stall floor with water from the shower head spraying their bodies like rain.

How was she going to manage without him? She would miss his effervescence, his joyous enthusiasm for life. In fact, she already did. He had helped her to understand how beautiful life could be. He had made her realize how closed, shallow and introverted her former life had been. She would never be the same again. He had touched a part of her that she hadn't known existed. And he had changed her. If she lived the rest of her life without him, his shadow would always follow her, reminding her to look at life his way, not hers.

Memories of Drake crowded her mind: the first day she'd met him, the day he'd brought the guitars to the orphanage to entertain the children, the crazy Christmas they'd celebrated in June with Drake's warm and wacky family, his understanding when she had told him the details of her mother's death. He had wanted to marry her despite everything. Drake had a gift for turning everything he touched to love.

And she'd thrown it all away when she walked out the door. Would he ever be able to forgive her? Could they ever be friends again?

It only there were a way to bury the past forever. Then she could give Drake all the love he deserved; all the love stored up in her heart. But unfortunately, that didn't seem possible. The past still held her like the victim she'd always been.

Impossible was a quitter's word. And she didn't like to think of herself as a quitter anymore. If Drake had shown her one thing about life, it was that running away from problems didn't solve anything. Carla reached out and with a quick twist, turned the water control to off. Then she stepped out of the shower.

As she toweled herself dry, she decided that it was time she had a talk with Dr. Cook. Maybe he could suggest a way out of her troubles. It was worth a try, anyway.

The drive north to Big Sur along the California coast is one of the most strikingly beautiful in the state. Unfortunately, Carla wasn't in the mood to enjoy the view. She barely noticed the high rocky cliffs that ended abruptly where they met the blue waters of the Pacific Ocean.

She did notice the tortuous, narrow road that was packed with Saturday traffic. Every delay, every slow-moving car, made her want to scream with frustration. On a good day, the drive from Los Angeles to Big Sur took seven hours. Today, she figured she'd be lucky if she made it in ten.

Carla pulled into Big Sur at eight o'clock that evening, feeling weary and burned out. Big Sur was a small town, known for its lofty redwood trees and reclusive-yet-famous artists and writers.

The only address she had for Dr. Cook was Pacific Grove, Big Sur. Noticing a small café, Carla stopped, got out and tied Lady Catherine to the fender of her car. "You wait here and I'll go get us some burgers and hopefully, some directions."

The café was small and self-consciously funky—the kind of place that uses alfalfa sprouts on its hamburgers instead of lettuce. All the tables were filled with people, but spotting an empty stool at the counter, Carla made her way across the room and sat down.

The service was slow, but at last a waitress dressed in tight blue jeans and a white peasant blouse appeared to take Carla's order. The girl seemed mildly surprised when Carla ordered two deluxe hamburgers with fries, but said nothing and soon disappeared into the kitchen. When the waitress eventually returned with her order, Carla said, "I'm here to visit a friend of mine, Dr. Cook. All I have for him as an address is Pacific Grove. Could you tell me where that is?"

The girl looked at her oddly, but was willing enough to give Carla directions. She was just about to walk away, when she turned and added, "You can't go there tonight. They lock the gates at seven o'clock."

Carla thanked her and soon left. After feeding Lady Catherine her dinner, she climbed back into her car and drove away.

Despite the waitress's warning, Carla decided to look for Dr. Cook's house. After taking several wrong turns, she finally found the narrow, winding road that led through the mountains and up to his house. Noticing the sturdy and tall white-painted steel fence that the waitress had described, Carla lifted her foot from the gas pedal to let the car slow down.

She came upon the gate, swung left, and stopped. Just as the waitress had warned, the gate was locked. On the gate was a sign that read Pacific Grove Temple of Enlightenment. Disciples Welcome from 9-2.

No wonder the waitress had looked at her oddly, Carla thought with a wry smile. Could Dr. Cook really be involved with this Temple of Enlightenment? What was it? And who were the disciples? It all sounded very strange.

Carla returned to Big Sur, found a motel, and collapsed in her bed. Tomorrow at nine she'd find out what the Pacific Grove Temple of Enlightenment was all about.

The next morning Carla awoke early, breakfasted at the same café she'd eaten at the previous night, then drove once again to the Temple of Enlightenment. When she arrived at the gates, she was relieved to discover them open this time.

The Temple of Enlightenment looked like a campground, Carla thought as she drove her car onto the property. The only building was a two-story redwood structure with sharp angles and many windows. Gathered around it were tents—at least thirty by Carla's quick count.

Carla parked her car and walked to the main building. As she entered through the front door, the smell of incense assaulted her senses. She saw a long hallway filled with sunshine from an overhead skylight. There was no furniture.

A dark-haired woman emerged from a door to Carla's right. She was dressed in a long gown of flowing lavender cotton gauze. "Good morning," she greeted pleasantly, walking toward Carla.

"Good morning," Carla replied. "I'm here to see Dr. Cook. He's an old friend."

"The Enlightened One is meditating at the moment," the woman said in a singsong voice. "He cannot be disturbed."

"I see," Carla said thoughtfully, although she didn't really see at all. "Look, I've driven all the way from Los Angeles to see Dr. Cook. It's extremely important. Couldn't you just tell him that Carla Fox is here to see him?" Carla looked at the woman with pleading eyes.

"I cannot interrupt him when he's meditating. But he'll be finishing in a few minutes. I'll tell him you're here then, though I make no promises whether he'll see you or not." The woman bowed, then turned and left the room.

There was no place to sit, so Carla paced instead. When she heard footsteps at last, she turned.

"Carla, it's good to see you," Dr. Cook said, walking toward her. His tall, thin body was clad in a white cotton-gauze robe similar to the woman's.

"Dr. Cook, h-how are you?" Carla stammered.

"Serene," Dr. Cook said placidly.

Carla looked at him, trying to hide the surprise she felt. The last time she had seen Dr. Cook he'd been dressed in a Brooks Brothers suit and tie. Today, the only recognizable feature of his old self was the shaggy inverted V of gray eyebrows over his brown eyes.

"Would you care for a carrot juice?" he asked with a melodramatic sweep of his hand. The diaphanous material of his robe fluttered as he moved. "I'm sorry I can't offer you anything stronger, but here at Pacific Grove we take a vow to give up the vices of the flesh."

"No, thanks. I'm fine," Carla replied. She was in a state of befuddlement. She'd come to ask Dr. Cook how he'd feel about her revealing the true details of her mother's death. She loved Drake, she needed Drake, but she would never feel free to love him properly with this cloud from the past hanging over her head. But Dr. Cook seemed so different. He wasn't the same man at all. She didn't know what to say to him.

"Why don't you come with me," Dr. Cook kindly suggested, seeming to notice her uneasy state of mind. "This is hardly the place for a private talk."

Carla followed him out of the building, up a steep path to a green nylon tent overlooking the compound. Dr. Cook stopped, unzipped the tent's flap, then stood aside and motioned for Carla to enter.

"How cozy," Carla nervously said, her eyes taking in the old orange crate neatly stacked with white robes, and a canvas cot covered with a sleeping bag. She took a step in, then sat down and asked him abruptly, "How long have you been here?"

"Time passage is different with us up here," Dr. Cook replied, sitting cross-legged on the floor next to

Carla. "By your time measure, I suppose it must be nearly four years."

"I see," Carla said, staring blankly at the wall of the canvas tent. She wished she could think of something more original to say. "I gather you're no longer practicing as a psychiatrist?"

"I've given up that tedious and shallow life. I went into psychiatry wanting to help mankind, but I soon discovered that everything I did was false. That's why I founded the Temple of Enlightenment. Nowadays, I really help people where they need it: spiritually."

"Oh, how nice," Carla remarked, not knowing what to say.

"You had something to do with this," Dr. Cook said. "I never recovered from the guilt I felt over what happened to you. You see, I'd suspected your mother of beating you for years, but I was afraid, both for my practice and my materialistic way of life. So I didn't do anything to help you, and let the years roll by. Then your mother died and you called on me for assistance. I lied to the police, hoping to protect you and ease my conscience. I suppose I was trying to help you, but later, when you came to me and told me of your nightmares, I wondered if I hadn't made things worse. It must have been a terrible burden for you to keep that secret all these years."

"It wasn't a burden," Carla lied. Her hands stroked the rough fibers of the canvas floor of the tent as she added, "Anyway, it doesn't matter. I've been happy as a social worker."

"I wish I could believe you, but I can't. I was a trained psychiatrist; I should have known that no one can be happy living a lie. Certainly, I wasn't happy. And how must it have been for you, just a young and innocent girl? You gave up music—the one thing you loved dearly—because of my lie. I never forgave myself for that. There were so many times when I wished I could confess it all. But I just didn't dare. I had you to think of. I had you to protect."

Carla looked at him, noticing the new lines of worry about his face. Still, there was a peaceful look in his eyes she hadn't seen before. He may have found an unconventional answer to his problem, but it seemed to have worked. "Dr. Cook," she said, "you mustn't feel guilty. You did what you felt was right. Anyway, I'm back into music. I'm doing a concert at the Hollywood Bowl tomorrow night."

Dr. Cook took Carla's hands in his and gripped them tightly. "Oh, I'm glad, really glad to hear that. A talent like yours should not be lost to the world."

"There's only one thing," Carla said, deciding to make a clean breast of the whole subject at once. "How would you feel if I were to reveal the true story to the police and the press?"

"If that was what you wanted to do, that would make me very happy," Dr. Cook said, clasping her hands even tighter. "You see the simple way I live here. I'm beyond the trappings of the world nowadays. Nothing anyone does can hurt or touch me. And quite frankly, I've wanted the truth known for years."

She looked at him with searching eyes. "Are you sure? You're not just saying that? The police and press might want to talk to you. It might not be easy."

"They can't hurt me. They can't touch me," he said confidently. "But do what you think best. I've already interfered in your life more than I should have."

"Okay," Carla said, rising from the floor. "And thank you ever so much."

Chapter Thirteen

Everything and anything that could possibly go wrong had gone wrong. Heavy fog had caused a four-car pileup that had brought traffic to a standstill on the road leading from Big Sur to Los Angeles. Carla sat in her car for nearly two hours, her nerves screaming with impatience to get moving.

The concert was tonight. If she was going to make it by eight o'clock, she couldn't afford to lose any more time. Carla looked at her watch and groaned. Twelve o'clock and she hadn't even passed the town of San Simeon yet.

Finally the traffic began to move again. Carla let out a sigh of relief. Then, not thirty miles later, Carla's Honda, which had always been as faithful as the famed Yellowstone Monument, died a sudden, noisy and horrible death.

It took an hour for the AAA Club to come and tow her car away. Leaving her car at a local garage with instructions to repair it, Carla rented another car and was gone.

She raced back to Los Angeles as fast as she could on the slow-moving road. The sun, a glowing ball of orange, red, yellow and purple haze, was already starting to descend below the horizon when she arrived in Los Angeles. Carla, who felt exhausted but keyed up, kept the speedometer needle firmly planted on seventy as she guided the car toward her home in Eagle Rock. It was too bad she hadn't thought to bring her black dress with her so she didn't have to backtrack all the way to Eagle Rock.

What would Drake say when he heard the good news—that she was finally free of her past. Would he be happy and take her in his arms and still want to marry her? Or would he be angry with her for walking out on him?

And what if her performance was a bomb? What if she made a complete fool of herself in front of all those people? She wouldn't just make herself look a fool, she'd make Drake look bad, too. Drake claimed that she still sang well, but he was prejudiced in her favor. Times had changed, and so had the fans and music critics. Would they agree with him?

She sighed despondently and looked at her watch. There was only an hour and a half left until the concert began. She'd have to change in a hurry to get there in time. If she made it in time....

* * *

Sunday night at the Hollywood Bowl. The evening air was so thick with smog that no stars shone in the charcoal-gray sky overhead. The air felt as hot and dry as Carla's throat. She coughed, hoping to relieve the parched, tight feeling that suffocated her, wondering if she was physically fit enough to sing tonight. If she had any sense at all, she'd turn around and leave right now.

As she wheeled her car into the parking lot, she could see and hear that the warm-up band had already started to perform. Carla nodded to the parking-lot attendant as she was waved toward the back part of the lot. Terrific, she thought to herself. Just what I need. The concert's already started and there's no place to park.

At last she found a place to park, in the far corner of the lot. As she got out of the car, she was relieved to hear that the warm-up band was still performing. Good. Drake and his brothers hadn't started to play yet.

As she stumbled along the asphalt driveway in her stiletto high heels, she thanked goodness that L.A. was a town where blue jeans and evening gowns were equally fashionable. None of the other latecomers walking toward the amphitheater seemed to take much notice of her in her long black velvet gown and high heels. The sound of laughter permeated the still air.

She got to the front gate, but she didn't have a ticket. Performers didn't need tickets to their own concerts; they went in the back way. Unfortunately, Carla hadn't the vaguest idea where that was, and since she didn't have the time to find it, she decided she'd have to enter as a fan.

Her eyes scanned the crowd, looking for a scalper with a ticket to sell. She spotted a man standing back from the crowd, a ticket held high over his head.

He was scruffy and looked as though he hadn't changed his clothes or cut his hair in a year. She hurried over to him and demanded tersely, "How much?"

"Well, let me see," he said thoughtfully, scratching his beard as he eyed her low-cut gown and the rope of pearls around her neck. "How about $500?"

"You've got to be kidding," Carla said contemptuously, suddenly remembering with dismay that she had very little cash on her. The trip to Big Sur had expended all her ready resources. She had twenty dollars on her at the most, and that would mean counting out dimes and quarters. She suggested, "How about twenty dollars?"

"Now you're the one who's kidding, lady," the man said, raising his hand to show his ticket to the crowd. "They cost me more'n that to buy."

Carla opened her evening bag and desperately began to search through her wallet for something, anything to appease the man. "Do you take Visa or American Express?"

"Sure, lady," he said, rolling his eyes to the heavens and starting to walk away.

"Wait, don't go," Carla said frantically, grabbing his arm. "I've got to have that ticket. How about an I.O.U.? I promise I'm good for it. I'll personally deliver the cash anywhere you want tomorrow."

"Yeah, right." He looked through the crowd for another customer. "You may be dressed up in that fancy dress and them pearls, but that don't mean nothing."

"My pearls. Of course, how could I be so stupid!" Carla exclaimed, her hands going to the clasp at the back of her neck. Her fingers unfastened the catch, as she added, "Here, take them, they're yours."

"What do I need fake pearls for?" the man scoffed, his eyes scanning the thinning crowd.

"But they're real! I swear they are!" Carla exclaimed. They were easily worth a small fortune, but she didn't care. What use did she have for pearls? All she needed was Drake. She stuffed the necklace into the man's hand, urging, "Take them, I beg of you. Please! I have to have that ticket."

"Well, okay, ma'am," the man agreed. "But if they ain't real I'm going to be mighty upset."

Carla grabbed the ticket from his hand. Then she turned and melted into the crowd.

The Hollywood Bowl was an open-air amphitheater with tiered concrete floors sloping down toward the stage. Over the stage was a rounded half-shell. Behind it loomed the Beachwood Canyon foothills with its rocky, dry, brown soil and rugged chaparral plants.

Carla emerged at the top of the theatre. Below her stretched yards and yards of people and concrete walkways. She looked at her watch. Only a few minutes until Drake and his brothers were scheduled to begin. She'd have to hurry.

"Excuse me, excuse me," she said, as her hands nudged and prodded the people in front of her. She glanced at her watch once again as her long slender legs ate up the distance. Damn! she swore to herself. There was only one more minute left until Drake would appear. "Excuse me, excuse me," she pleaded, pushing aside everyone in her way. She had to get down to the stage immediately.

She almost made it. If it hadn't been for the security guard stationed at the bottom row of seats, she would have. But she'd forgotten about the guards.

"Oh, no, you don't," a man in a khaki-colored uniform said, as he reached out an arm to stop her. He was tall and slender, with blond hair, a mustache and a gold badge pinned to his shirt. There was a gun in the holster at his hip.

"You don't understand!" Carla breathlessly said, trying to break his hold on her. "I'm Carla Fox. I'm supposed to be on that stage."

"Sure, you're Carla Fox," the guard said. "And I'm Drake Lanning. Now, why don't you go sit down and behave yourself? Drake will be performing soon."

"But I am Carla Fox. Really I am. And I can prove it," she said, opening her purse and searching for her wallet. Flipping open the wallet, she showed him her driver's license. "See?"

Leaning over, the officer looked at her picture and the name on her license. "It says here your name's Carla Foster, not Carla Fox."

"That's what I call myself these days," Carla explained impatiently, her heart beating faster from nervous tension. "Haven't you seen my picture in the papers or on TV?"

"I work the night shift. I don't have time for that," the policeman replied. "Now, why don't you come with me and we'll have a nice and quiet little concert in the squad car?"

"But I am Carla Fox," she protested. "Look at me. Don't you recognize me?"

He tried to pull her away, but Carla let her body go limp, a dead weight. She fell against him, pleading. "Please, officer, look at me! I'm Carla Fox. You must recognize me!"

By this time, a couple of curious onlookers had gathered around them. Carla straightened up, saying desperately, "Come on, one of you must know me. Tell this man I'm Carla Fox!"

"I can see a resemblance," a man in preppy plaid Bermuda shorts and a green Ixod shirt said. "But it's hard to tell from just a picture. You might be Carla Fox and you might not."

"You've got to believe me," Carla said urgently. "Why do you think I'm all dressed up like this? I'm supposed to be on the stage singing any moment."

"We'll discuss all of this later at the station," the guard said pulling out handcuffs. "I'm sorry, ma'am, but if you won't go quietly, I'll have to arrest you."

"No, please!" Carla cried, her eyes darting from one person to another. "Someone say you know me!"

"It seems to me there's only one way to really prove to us who you really are," said a tall woman. "Why don't you sing for us? We may not recognize your face, but your voice we'd know in an instant."

The man in the plaid Bermuda shorts agreed. "Yeah, sing for us. That'll show us who you really are."

Carla's gaze swung to the officer. "Please, give me one minute more. I promise I'll go quietly if no one recognizes my voice."

He seemed to consider it a moment, looking at her expectant face. "Okay," he said. "And then, if you don't go quietly, I'll have to escort you out of here."

"I promise," Carla agreed. Taking a deep breath, she began to sing.

"That's Carla Fox!" the woman said. "I'd know her voice anywhere."

"You're right," the man agreed. "That *is* Carla Fox. You've got to let her go, Officer. She's supposed to be on that stage any second now."

The officer still looked doubtful. Carla wondered if she should try to make a break for it. To be this close and to fail—it was too frustratingly ironic! She watched as the policeman pulled out a walkie-talkie attached to his belt and lifted it to his mouth.

"Tippet here," he said. "I've got a small problem..."

It was at that moment that Drake Lanning and his band walked onto the stage. The crowd immediately went wild, standing up and shouting and waving. Anything that Officer Tippet might have said was drowned out by the noise around them.

Carla thought Drake looked marvelous as he walked onto the stage. He was wearing tight-fitting white jeans slung low on his lean, muscular hips. His very thin white linen shirt clung to his body so closely that

Carla could see the outline of his lithe torso and the dark shadow of body hair running from his waist to his throat. The shirt was open as far as his sternum, the lapels back, exposing his smooth, tanned skin. A guitar was gripped in his right hand. Waving to the crowd, he stepped up to the microphone and gestured for the audience to be quiet.

"Good evening. I'm glad all of you could make it here tonight," Drake said, trying to be heard over the noise. It was a futile gesture for most of the deliriously excited audience, but Carla, who was only a few yards away, could hear him quite well. She watched him brush the familiar drooping lock of hair away from his face. She saw the gleam of his dark eyes and the wide expanse of white teeth as he smiled. If only she hadn't been so afraid, she might be up there with him now. He'd know how much he meant to her if she could only sing to him.

Carla cast a glance at Officer Tippet, whose attention was now diverted to the stage. Carefully, she began to back away from him. Arcing her eyes around her to see if anyone else had noticed her cautious retreat, she noticed that the tall woman was watching her. The woman smiled and nodded for her to go. Carla needed no more encouragement. She turned on her heels and ran. The woman stepped forward to block Officer Tippet's way.

Carla thanked the person who had invented slits for tight-fitting evening dresses. The one in hers greatly facilitated her ability to run the few remaining yards to the stage. Waving her arms frantically to attract attention, she called Drake's name as loudly as she could.

Oblivious to Carla's movements, Drake raised his hands in a gesture calling for the crowd to silence, then waited for them to calm down. He leaned over the microphone and said, "I've got some good news and some bad news. The good news is that I'm here. The bad news is that—"

"Drake, Drake, I'm right here!" Carla screamed, hoping desperately that she would be able to be heard now that the crowd had quieted. She was standing just a few feet away from Drake, but the stage was a good six feet above the ground. She would never be able to climb up that tall wall without his assistance.

Whether he heard her or just happened to look down, she didn't know or care. But he did look down, and a grin split his face when he saw her in the long black evening gown, waving her hands frantically. Walking to the edge of the stage, he squatted down on his knees and set his guitar on the floor. Then he bent over, offered Carla a hand and pulled her up. Softly, for her ears only, he said, "It's about time, beautiful. I'd about given up on you."

Drake retrieved his guitar from the stage, then stood up and, taking Carla's hand in his, walked back to the microphone. The crowd, who had seen her unusual entrance, was remarkably quiet. Still, they didn't hear Drake's softly murmured "Steady, Carla. You're going to be great." But they did hear Drake say into the microphone. "The bad news folks, is that Miss Carla Fox was almost late. I think I'm going to have to dock her time card.'' The audience promptly broke into laughter at his joke.

At first, the sea of faces staring up at Carla was frightening. It had been so long since she'd been before a crowd. For a fleeting moment she remembered the last time she'd been in front of an audience, then she sternly blacked that depressing memory out of her head. And then Bobby, who'd been standing at the back with the rest of the band, came forward. His saxophone solo was to begin the first song. She heard him whisper, ''Let's kill 'em, Carla,'' and then he started to play a sad, haunting refrain. Carla's cue was next. Taking a deep breath, she stepped over to the microphone and began to sing.

Thousands of fans couldn't be wrong. The Drake Lanning-Carla Fox concert was a rousing success. Carla left the stage that night feeling elated, exhausted and keyed up. And very proud of herself. She'd done it. She'd confronted the ghosts of her past and stared them down.

''I appreciate your showing up tonight,'' Drake said, his eyes watching her carefully as they walked off the stage after their fifth encore. ''You really had me worried for a while. I was sure you weren't going to show up.''

''I know,'' Carla said, raising her eyes to his. ''I'm sorry I ran away. I needed time to think and to be alone with myself for a while.'' Linking her arm into his, she added, ''Drake, we need to talk. Let's get out of here.''

He opened his mouth to respond, but a sudden brilliant glare of light and the sound of flashbulbs popping stopped him. Momentarily blinded, Carla blinked her eyes instinctively against the bright lights. She heard Drake say under his breath, "If you're quick you can miss this gang of reporters. I'll stall them until you can get away."

Carla kept her hand planted on Drake's arm possessively. She lifted her chin proudly. She was done with running away and she wanted him to know it. "Thanks, but no thanks. I'll talk to them, if you don't mind."

Carla picked up the morning newspaper and reread the review of the concert with mixed feelings of joy, disgust and depression. She should be thrilled about the kudos she'd received from the entertainment editor. He was well-known for deriding the best of performances. A good review from him was considered more meaningful than a Grammy. And the review had been good.

Cynic that I am, I've been proclaiming for years that any singer can make a hit out of a good song. I'd like to take those smug words of mine back. Last night I heard Carla Fox sing for the first time in ten years. I now stand corrected, and if it's possible—humbled. Be it ever so unusual, there's nothing like talent. And Carla Fox has plenty of it.

When I first heard about this proposed concert of Drake Lanning and Carla Fox, I laughed outright. I thought the idea of pairing two such disparate performers sounded like a one-way ticket to boredom—an instant disaster.

But, from the moment that Drake and Carla stepped on that stage and began to sing, I knew I was wrong...and very lucky. A performance with last night's intensity comes rarely in a performer's lifetime. The amount of electricity those two put out last night beats Southern California Edison's output for a year.

Sometimes the perks of this job aren't half bad. Who would have known that Drake Lanning and Carla Fox would make performing history last night? I didn't. I couldn't have guessed it. But now I know. And I can't wait to hear what the two of them will do next. Put me down on the waiting list of fans eagerly anticipating an album or another concert.

Wanna know a secret? I'd even be willing to put out my own hard-earned cash for the next concert. Just don't tell my editor that. *He*'d make me do it.

Carla put down the newspaper and stifled a big yawn. The clock read 7:00 a.m., and she hadn't been to bed yet. She'd waited up all night hoping that Drake would show up at her house. Her wait had been in vain.

She got up from the couch, stretched her arms, and yawned once again, deciding that she might as well try to get some sleep. Obviously, Drake wasn't going to show up. She padded into the bedroom, where Lady

Catherine was already asleep in her favorite spot under the bed.

"Even you deserted me in my hour of need," Carla accused the sleeping dog as she pulled off her sleek blue silk caftan. As she hung the caftan neatly on a hanger, she noted gloomily that Drake had wrought more than just a few minor changes in her personality; here she was hanging up her clothing. She never used to do that.

In the back of her closet she found her favorite pink pajamas. They were made of a thin cotton material with see-through crocheted lace on the square yoke and cuffs. Although old and well-worn, Carla couldn't bear to throw this pair of pajamas out. Every time a seam gave way, she carefully repaired it.

The pajamas felt soft and soothing against her bare skin as she climbed into bed. She was wrapped in her own special security blanket. Pulling the covers over her body, Carla closed her eyes and tried to drift off to sleep. But sleep could be as elusive as love; whenever she had looked for it, she could never find it.

Her mind kept returning to what had happened the previous night. The swarm of well-wishers and reporters had soon managed to separate her from Drake. When she had finally gotten a chance to look for him, he'd disappeared. Where had he gone? Why hadn't he come to visit her? He could have at least called. After all, she'd told him she wanted talk to him. Was he still so angry that he wouldn't even allow her the dignity of one final conversation?

The concert was history. Tomorrow's future was waiting. But it all stretched empty and useless without Drake. He had worked his way under her skin and into her heart. He had changed her. The prospect of returning to the orphanage no longer held much appeal. She still cared about the kids; she still wanted to help and do for them. But now she realized that she needed more out of life: she needed music. It seemed that she had come full circle. She wanted to perform again.

One of the well-wishers she'd met had been a recording-studio executive who'd offered her a record contract at an exorbitant amount of money. She was considering accepting the offer. If she threw herself into work, it might help her forget her pain.

Carla had thought that she'd felt as much pain as any one person could endure in a lifetime. But she'd been wrong; losing Drake was far worse than anything she'd ever known before.

Her mind was still racing when she heard the doorbell. She considered not answering it. Most likely it was just another reporter who had managed to find her address. There'd been a couple of them waiting on her doorstep when she'd gotten home from the concert. Although she had decided to no longer shun reporters and publicity, there was no reason to invite them into the privacy of her home.

Nevertheless, she climbed out of bed and padded barefoot toward the front door, deciding she'd just take a look and see who it was.

She stuck an eye to the peephole and saw Drake standing on the stoop. Her heart gave a quick lurch. Hurriedly, she opened the door.

"Hello, Drake," she said with false brightness, stepping aside so that he could enter the house. "Won't you come in? I'm sorry I'm such a mess, but I wasn't expecting you at this hour."

She looked nervous, Drake thought as he stepped into the room. And cute. Her pajamas made her look years younger than she was. She looked sexy and small and fragile. He wanted to take her in his arms immediately, but he resisted the urge. For once in his life he was going to follow his own advice and not rush her.

"Would you like a drink?" Carla asked a trifle breathlessly, searching for some way she could go back to her room and change into something more appropriate... and alluring.

"It's 8:00 a.m.," Drake reminded her gently as his brown eyes regarded her with amusement. "I think I'll pass this time."

"So it is," Carla said, her gaze arcing the room. Her housekeeping might have improved considerably, thanks to his influence, but it wasn't perfect yet. Scooping up the previous night's discarded panty hose from the couch, she crumpled them into a ball and hid them behind her back, asking, "Well, how about some coffee? Yes, that sounds like a good idea. I'll go make some coffee." She started to dash toward the kitchen door.

"If I wanted coffee I'd have gone to a coffee shop," Drake said, catching her arm and stopping her. "Why don't we sit down? You said last night that you wanted to talk to me. That's why I'm here. Let's talk."

"Why, yes, I did want to talk to you," she stammered, looking around for a place to sit. Cramming the panty hose underneath her, she sank down on the couch. Drake settled himself next to her. "I wanted to thank you for going to all that trouble over the concert. It was really nice of you. The kids are extremely grateful. I expect you'll be getting thank-you letters in the mail from them soon." She paused, realizing she was rambling, and waited for Drake to say something back. He just sat there watching her with amused amber eyes, a faint grin tugging the corners of his mouth.

The long silence made her panic. "And, oh yes, Elizabeth has found us a new building. It's in Altadena and is just perfect! It's got lots of land and—" She stopped midsentence. Why was he smiling at her in that adorable, superior way? Didn't he know she found it annoying and absolutely irresistible? How dare he show up at her house looking so smug and sure of himself? He must know that she was in love with him. He must know that she was hurting. Didn't he care? Why was he here?

Drake said smoothly, "I'm glad to hear Elizabeth found a suitable building. I sent her a check for the rest of the money this morning. Is that all you wanted to talk to me about?"

"Well, no," Carla murmured. Smoothing the fabric on her pajamas, she said hesitantly, "Look, I'm—I'm sorry I ran out on you like that. It's just that Angie came by and said some things that kind of upset me."

"I know," he interjected gently. "She blew your cover. I'm sorry she did that, Carla. It was a mean and vindictive thing to do. I realize it's going to make life difficult for you in the future." He hesitated for a moment. "And, I realize she must have said some things about her and me, also. Carla, you have to believe that there is nothing between us anymore. As soon as you came into my life, I broke it off with her. We'd always been friends more than anything else, but I guess she read more into it than I realized. I guess she came back from her latest trip hoping to...work things out. I'm sorry if she hurt you."

Carla looked down at the floor. "I realized she was lying almost as soon as I left. But she had made me so upset, what with everything else that was going on. I know she was just pulling at straws. Anyway, the whole thing was good in the end." She gazed straight into his eyes. "It made me do something I should have done a long time ago."

"What's that?"

"Visit Dr. Cook." She flashed him a smile, and then began to laugh. Drake watched her in puzzlement until at last she managed to say, "Oh, Drake, I wish you could have been there. He's become guru-vy!"

"Groovy?" Drake repeated, still looking perplexed.

"No, gu-ru-vy," Carla corrected him, enunciating the syllables carefully. "You see, you've got the spelling all wrong. It's spelled *g-u-r-u-v-y*. Guru-vy."

"Carla, you're not making any sense," Drake said, flicking back the curl drooping over his forehead.

Carla stopped him with a smirk and a raised hand. "You're not listening. That's why you don't understand. Dr. Cook's become a guru! I visited him in Big Sur. He's now the leader of the Pacific Grove Temple of Enlightenment, disciples welcome from nine to two!''

"Carla, what's gotten into you? You're not making any sense.''

"I'm making perfect sense for the first time in years," Carla explained with exultation. "Dr. Cook has forsaken the material world. He's become a guru! He's given up the sins of the flesh and now lives in a tent. The day I visited him he even offered me a glass of carrot juice!''

"But why did you visit him?" Drake asked. "That was so long ago. It was such a painful memory.''

"I went to Dr. Cook to ask him to let me tell the truth of what happened so many years ago," Carla explained. "I knew that was the only way we could ever be really happy together." Carla spread out her arms joyfully, turned to Drake and gave him a big hug. "Don't you understand? I'm free of the past! I can say anything I want. I can do anything I want. Dr. Cook has forsaken the material world. Nothing I can say or do will ever hurt him.''

"Carla, that's great news," Drake said, hugging her back. He pushed her away abruptly and looked at her searchingly. "But where does that leave me—and us?''

"That's for you to decide," she replied, her clear blue eyes suddenly serious and pleading. "I love you. I realize I'm not always such an easy person to love back. But you've got to understand. I'd been unhappy for so long that I didn't know how to handle being happy. But I do now—if you'll just give me one more chance.''

"So you want another chance, do you?" he asked, dragging her back into his arms. She felt his lips nuzzle in her hair, felt his hands slide underneath her pajama top and caress her breasts.

"Please," Carla whispered as she lifted her head and found his lips. She pressed her mouth against his in a hungry, devouring kiss.

Reluctantly, Drake pulled away. Carla looked at him in surprise, her eyes still hazy with passion. Although a smile creased the sharply chiseled planes of his face, his eyes were dark and enigmatic. "You'll marry me, won't you." He said it as a statement, not as a question.

"Yes, of course," she agreed with a happy smile and a tiny nod of assent.

"Then you'd better hurry up and get changed. The plane leaves in an hour."

"The plane?" she queried with a puzzled frown. "What plane?"

"The plane I chartered yesterday to take us to Reno today to get married."

Carla's blue eyes frosted. "The plane you chartered *yesterday*? How could you have known yesterday that I would agree to marry you today?"

"I didn't know, but I was hoping," he admitted, standing up. He grabbed one of Carla's hands and pulled her up with him. "That's why I hedged on the bet. I hired a plane big enough to fly the whole Lanning family. Oh, yes, Elizabeth's coming to. I figured you might be willing to disappoint me, but not the rest of the crew. They're waiting for us at the airport right now."

"They're waiting for us at the airport right now," Carla repeated, her voice rising sharply. "Why didn't you warn me? Why didn't you tell me about this last night?"

"I wanted to surprise you," Drake said, having trouble containing his smile.

"You wanted to surprise me!" she cried irately, backing away from him. "You mean railroad me. Of all the dirty, underhanded, blackmailing tricks—"

"Carla, you talk too much," Drake interrupted impatiently. "Do you want to marry me or don't you?"

"Of course I want to marry you!" she shouted.

"Then why are you angry? Why are you complaining?"

"I don't know!" she yelled. "I guess it's the way you do things. You're so doggone bossy!"

"Carla, shut up," he interrupted, catching her suddenly and raining kisses on her eyelids, her lips and her hair. "I promise, this is the last time I'll ever boss you around. Now go get dressed. Immediately."

"Yes, sir," she said demurely, glancing at him briefly as she walked out of the room. A smile curved her full lips. She knew he would never be able to keep that promise of not bossing her around.

Nevertheless it was a happy marriage. *A very happy marriage.*

* * * * *

COMING NEXT MONTH

#409 A CERTAIN SMILE—Lynda Trent
Impulsive widow Megan Wayne and divorced father Reid Spencer didn't have
marriage in mind, but what harm could come if their friendship turned into
something stronger? Reid's two teenage daughters didn't intend to let them
find out....

#410 FINAL VERDICT—Pat Warren
Prosecutor Tony Adams's upbringing had built him a strong case against lasting
love. Could attorney Sheila North's evidence to the contrary weaken his
defenses and free his emotions from solitary confinement?

#411 THUNDERSTRUCK—Pamela Toth
Crew member Honey Collingsworth accepted the risks of hydroplane racing.
Still, when her brother and dashing defector Alex Checkhov competed,
churning up old hatred, she feared for their lives...and her heart.

#412 RUN AWAY HOME—Marianne Shock
Proud landowner Burke Julienne knew that to restless vagabond
Savannah Jones, the lush Julienne estate was just another truck stop. Yet
he found her mesmerizing, and he prayed that one day Savannah would trade
freedom for love.

#413 A NATURAL WOMAN—Caitlin Cross
When farmer's daughter Vana Linnier abruptly became a sophisticated
celebrity, she desperately needed some plain old-fashioned horse sense to cope
with her jealous sister and her disapproving but desirable boss, Sky Van Dusen.

#414 BELONGING—Dixie Browning
Saxon Evanshaw returned home to a host of family fiascos and the lovely but
stealthy estate manager, Gale Chandler. Who was she really? Where were the
missing family treasures? And would Gale's beauty rob him of his senses?

AVAILABLE THIS MONTH:

#403 SANTIAGO HEAT
Linda Shaw

#404 SOMETIMES A MIRACLE
Jennifer West

#405 CONQUER THE MEMORIES
Sandra Dewar

#406 INTO THE SUNSET
Jessica Barkley

#407 LONELY AT THE TOP
Bevlyn Marshall

#408 A FAMILY OF TWO
Jude O'Neill

Starting in October...

SHADOWS ON THE NILE

by

Heather Graham Pozzessere

A romantic short story in six installments from best-selling author Heather Graham Pozzessere.

The first chapter of this intriguing romance will appear in all Silhouette titles published in October. The remaining five chapters will appear, one per month, in Silhouette Intimate Moments' titles for November through March '88.

Don't miss *Shadows on the Nile*—a special treat, coming to you in October. Only from Silhouette Books.

Be There!

IMSS-1